Where Monsoons Cry

For
Steve

" We are shaped and fashioned
by what we love."
— Goethe

I hope you enjoy these stories —
Perhaps inspire you to visit India.
With warm regards,
Lalita

Where Monsoons Cry

stories
by

Lalita Noronha

A Do The Write Thing Book
www.blackwordsonline.com/Monsoon.htm

Published by BlackWords Press
PO Box 21, Alexandria, VA 22313

Do The Write Thing, BlackWords Press and the portrayal of
the Fist with the Pencil are trademarks of BlackWords, Inc.

Publisher: Kwame Alexander
Cover & Book Design: Do The Write Thing
Cover Photo: David Hare
Text Artwork: Ann R. Oster

ISBN 1-888018-32-1
LCCN: 2004111849

First Edition:
Printed in the United States of America
1 3 5 7 9 10 8 6 4 2

Some of the stories in this collection have appeared elsewhere in modified form:
"Reunion" in *Potomac Review*, "Half and Half" in *Wordwrights*, "Running" and "The
Barren Window Ledge" in *The Baltimore Review*, "Lady in White" in *A Thousand Worlds:
An Anthology of Indian Women Writers*, Aurat Books, ed. Husta and Nellore, and in *Lite
Circle*, "Touch the Moon" in *BrickStreet*, and versions of "This is America" in *Tapestries*,
and "Deep Wells" in *The Asian Pacific Journal* and *Reed Magazine*. "This is America,"
"Almost a Son," "Under the Gul-Mohur Tree," "Lilacs" and "Peacock Dance" were pub-
lished in chapbook form as part of the 1997 *Maryland Short Story Literary Award*.

For my family: Larry, Jonathan and Anjali

and

In memory of my friend:
MaryAnn Suehle

III

I

"THE same lotus of our clime blooms here in the alien water with the same sweetness, under another name."
-Rabindranath Tagore

THIS IS AMERICA

I knock on his office door, wait, then push it open gently. Dr. Barrett looks up from a stack of papers. Like my father, he too, is fifty something, slightly weathered, still imposing, with a little red mark on the bridge of his nose, the size of a pinhead.

"Excuse me, Sir, may I come in?"

He pushes his glasses up and smiles generously. "Ah! Yes, come in." He tilts his chair, laces his fingers behind his head. "Certainly. And you don't have to call me Sir."

I enter, my black binder and the *Principles of Physics,* by Miller and Campbell, tucked under my arm. Behind him, the campus lawns are lush green, the hedges trimmed in graceful curving arches. The window is ajar despite a nip in the air. He is wearing a cream shirt and tan slacks. A lightweight brown jacket is draped over the back of his chair. "Do you have a moment, Sir?"

He looks at his wrist. "Sure. Twenty minutes before my next class. Your name?"

"Prem. Premila Ramachandran," I say, unfolding my test on

vectors. "I don't quite understand this."

"You mean the problems?" he asks, taking the test from me.

"Yes, some of them." I hand him a blue sheet of paper with rows of letters and numbers on it. "Like here, I wanted to explain how I got my answer, but there's no space."

"No, no," he interrupts, "You work it out in your head or in the test margin, then shade in the answer. It's called multiple choice."

"Multiple choice? Sounds confusing, Sir. Besides, number 13 has no answer. None of the choices fits." Little crow lines appear near his eyes. My eyes begin to sting as if I'm chopping onions. "I'm used to essays."

His mouth bursts open in a loud guffaw. "Essays? In physics?" Laughter rolls from his throat in waves. "Holy shit! That's priceless." He takes a handkerchief from his pocket, wipes his eyes, and hands back my test. "Sit down, Prem," he says, pushing some books aside.

I take my time, biting the inside of my mouth raw. Mercifully, the phone rings.

"Hal Barrett. Physics." His voice turns crisp, dry, business-like.

I look out the window and concentrate on a dangling red maple leaf. The veins are translucent in the sunlight, the burgundy pigment rich and sheer like my *tussore* silk *sari* with filigree leaves. On a bench, a boy in a gray sweatshirt, the letters CDU emblazoned across the front, pores over a book. Above him, the trellis is draped in brown, clematis blooms gone, the vine dead. Dr. Barrett's voice crackles sharply into the receiver.

"Hmm. Hmm. What? Seven in the morning, did you say?" He shakes his head. "I'm tenured, remember? And I've been Physics Chair for the last four years. My eyeballs are barely open at that hour." He pauses, tapping his fingers on the desk. "Oh, all right. Fine." He hangs up. "Assholes," he mutters under his breath absently and turns to me. His eyes soften. "Look. I'm in a hurry now, but I'm free Tuesdays at two. Why don't you come for help?"

"Sir, I couldn't," I blurt out. "My stipend is $240 a month."

"Oh! No, no money."

"Tuition for free? Sir, I couldn't—"

"Just come, Prem," he says, "okay? We'll see."

This is my first month in America the beautiful, my first semester in graduate school. But I've been found deficient in Physics, Chemistry, Math, and so must acquire these skills. Mrs. Jenkins, the foreign student counselor, eyes me sharply. "It's a heavy course load, but it can be done," she says.

She is plump, fiftyish, very efficient, I can tell, by the way she puckers her mouth and drums her fingers on her desk. She takes a sip of coffee from a black mug with two pursed red lips flanking the handle, and the words "Kiss a pig" printed on the front."

"Your file is here, somewhere," she says, shuffling a sheaf of papers on her desk. "Ah, here it is!"

As she extracts my folder, a pink tuition remission card drifts like an autumn leaf and lands on her soft leather boots. Slowly, she picks it up and waves it mid-air. Her mouth twists in a small, sardonic smile. Something about her manner, perhaps the way her eyes wash over me, tells me she thinks America is for "Americans."

"As you know," she says, "we'll only pay for one year of make-up courses. If fourteen credits are too much. . ."

"Oh no, that's fine, Ma'am." I reassure her, eager to appear serious and intelligent, although I haven't the foggiest idea what "credit" means. I'm just grateful it's free. She smiles, satisfied, pushes her chair back to indicate our time is up.

Walking diagonally across the beautiful campus, I see trees splattered with vibrant colors I've never seen on trees before—chili red, turmeric yellow, *kesar* orange. A cool breeze catches under my *sari* and lifts it like a hot air balloon. Pulling it tight around my knees, I hurry past the football field, through the turnstile, to Mr. and Mrs. Malloy's house where I live. Tomorrow, I must wear the long cashmere sweater my mother knitted for me.

Later that evening, I write my first letter home.

> *Dear Ma:*
>
> *I understand now why America is the land of milk and honey. There is so much of everything here—wide open spaces, big houses, cars, money. I live near the college campus with a nice American family. The Malloys are kind despite their wealth. In the living room, there's a beautiful emerald green carpet, so plush that I walk barefoot just so my feet can sink in. And there's a crystal chandelier in the dining room above a mahogany table and satin cushioned chairs. The dining room is just for show. We eat in an alcove near a bay window in a cheery kitchen, which opens onto the patio. My room is in the attic, and I don't have to share my bathroom with anyone else. Oh, if you could see the shower! You turn it one way, the water comes out hot, the other way, and it's cold. No heating water on stoves, no clanging buckets; there are machines for everything—to wash dishes, grind leftovers, crush garbage, and in the basement, a "washer and dryer" for clothes. You're wondering what a basement is, right? It's like a house under the house, except that no one lives in it. The Malloys play billiards and keep their wine collection down there.*

My job is to wash the dishes and sweep the kitchen every night. Mornings, I get Jason and James ready for school; Mrs. Malloy takes Erica to Montessori. Saturdays, we go to a park nearby or play on campus. Living near school is convenient; I don't need a car that way. On Sundays, we go to Church together, and then Mr. Malloy fixes brunch—bacon, scrambled eggs, sausage links, tomato juice with vodka, but without fried onions and green chilies, the eggs taste bland and pasty. Sunday evenings, I'm free. That's when I wrap my hair in warm coconut oil and wash it with scented liquid soaps made for fine, dry or oily hair. In America there is a cure for everything.

Please write often. I miss home.

"Come in, come in, Prem," Dr. Barrett says, as if he's really glad to see me. I walk in, like always, Physics text under my arm. I am wearing a *salwar khameez* today, a leaf green one, with a high Chinese collar and embroidery down the front like a tree trunk, flowers fanning out in sprays over my breasts. Back home, forests are brown and green. My first boyfriend called me "forest girl" because I wore green—lime, chartreuse, mint, coriander-green. But here, outside Dr. Barrett's office, the trees stand bare and gray like old men.

"You seem far away," Dr. Barrett's voice is mildly reproachful.

I smile. "I'm sorry, Sir."

"What's that you're wearing?" he asks, as if he could read my thoughts.

"*Salwar khameez*, Sir. *Khameez* means shirt."

"Very pretty," he says, his eyes taking it all in. "Interesting costume."

"It's not really a costume, Sir. It's worn more in North India.

17

The *salwar* is tight, keeps the cold out." I stick my leg out to show him.

"Hmm," he says. "I've seen photographs of Nehru in those things."

"Yes, men wear them too."

We turn to chapter six, *"Trajectories and Projectile Movements."* I am nervous about tomorrow's test. I understand concepts but can't solve problems without calculus.

I tried once to explain my predicament to Mrs. Jenkins. "Dr. Corey says math precedes physics, Ma'am," I said, mouthing Dr. Corey's words. "Sequential course work."

Mrs. Jenkins eyed me like a beady lizard. She was wearing a winter white suit like the one Barbara Walters wore last week on *60 Minutes.* Her eye shadow was teal blue, her full mouth cherry red.

"That's true for our regular students." She walked over to her file cabinet and lifted my folder out. "But there's no time, no funds. Foreign students must make up deficiencies fast."

I told her that deficiencies are easier to make up in history or literature. She cut me off, glancing at my folder. "Look Miss, uh? Ramacha.." she said, glancing down again. She gave up on my last name. "I explained the system. If you drop physics ..."

"Please call me Prem, Ma'am," I interrupted, gently.

"Prem? That's pretty," she said.

I smiled. "It means love. All Indian names have a meaning, Ma'am."

She flipped a page. "I see. Look, I wish I could help," she said, "but the school only pays for two undergrad semesters. That's generous. After all, you're in graduate school, right?"

I nodded.

"You have a BS," she continued, tapping her painted finger-nail on the next line, "and an MS too!" Her voice, an octave higher was half surprised, half admiring.

"Yes, Ma'am. In ecology research. No math or physics was needed."

Mrs. Jenkin's heels clicked on the tile as she walked back to the file cabinet. "I'm sorry," she said. "There's nothing more I can do. If you want, you can transfer to another university..." Her voice trailed off as she disappeared behind a carton of boxes.

My heart stopped. Another university? What university? And how would I "transfer?" Quietly, I left her office and walked past the foyer, past the columns of pink granite holding up this beautiful edifice of learning. Standing on the top-most step, I looked down at cascading lawns, tall evergreens, steps winding down to terrace gardens sprinkled with buildings. How could I leave? Here, at least, I had a place to live near school; I didn't need a car. How would I get one? And who would teach me to drive? A "transfer" sounded terrifying. Besides, the Malloy children were sweet. They called me "our Indian—the wah, wah kind." They laughed, tapping their fingers over open mouths, putting feathers in their heads and dancing, wah-wah, around an imaginary fire. No, no, not Native American, I explained, pointing to India on their beautiful world globe with the polished chrome axes. See, I told them, it's a small country, only one third as big as America; almost easier to get there by boring a tunnel through the earth.

How could I start over? What would my mother say?

Dear Ma:

Let me explain the misunderstanding. No, I'm not a servant. Here, students work in people's houses, rake leaves, shovel snow, do odd jobs. My friend Janice gets paid to "house sit," which means she lives in someone's house and does nothing but feed the cat and water plants while the owners are away. It's a great job! The Malloy's don't pay me but I get a room, TV, food—all free! I don't pay electricity, not even phone bills unless I call long distance. But whom would I call? I even use their soap. Mrs. Malloy buys "Irish Spring" by the carton, so I take a few cakes up to my room. It smells like perfume.

School is fine except for Physics. Dr. Barrett, my Physics teacher, tutors me on Tuesdays but he doesn't charge because I have no money. Last month I bought a coat and winter boots. Once I pay off my book loans, I'll even be able to send money home. If you like, tell Auntie Celie that I live in the dormitory. There's no family disgrace that way."

I put down my pen and re-read my mother's small, slanted handwriting. "This whole thing is a mistake," I read. "Girls don't need to go to college in the first place, and certainly not in America. You should have got a job like your cousin, Beth. Your Auntie Celie thinks you're working there as a servant."

Waves of anger flood my cheeks. Walking into my sparkling white-tiled bathroom, I address the oak beveled mirror. "Give me a chance, will you? I know. I know girls don't go to college. But it'll pay off, damn it! You'll see!"

"You did better this time," Dr. Barrett says, glancing at my recent test on Trajectories.

"Thanks, Sir. I've been trying to read ahead in math."

"That's very good. You're smart," he says, "and terribly pretty."

I don't answer. Gathering my hair up, I twist it into a knot. Today, it is windy and cold; so windy, my braid came loose filling my hair with static electricity. Dr. Barrett picks a few loose strands from my face and tucks them behind my ear.

"Ouch," he says, laughing, as the electricity gets him. I laugh too. As always, he tilts his chair back and locks his fingers behind his neck. His eyes linger on my face for a moment. "You know, there's something about you that's just like her," he says.

"Like whom?"

Opening his top right hand desk drawer, he pulls out a photograph of a smiling woman with brown eyes and long, brown hair. Her teeth are even, pearl white, lips pink and parted.

"Oh! She's very beautiful," I exclaim.

Suddenly, his eyes turn to steel. "My wife. She's in Vietnam. She's a nurse," he says, his voice flat and expressionless.

"What's her name?"

"Celina."

"Celina? Oh, that's like a song. What does it mean?"

"Mean?" He returns the photograph to the drawer.

"Prem means love," I explain.

"Oh! Well, Celina means nothing," he says, drawing his lips in a thin line. "No meaning."

>Dear Ma:
>
>Today, I saw my first snow flake. I stood underneath a street lamp and stuck out my tongue and this cool powdery fluff fell all over my eyes and nose. It's almost Christmas. How beautiful the stores are! Bows, lights, real live pine trees, and carols everywhere— even in grocery stores. It's so different in a Christian land, not like home where Christmas means nothing to most people.
>
>My friend, Janice, invited me to her home in Maine but I declined. It's even colder there, plus it'll use up all my savings. Also, the Malloys asked me to stay. They have a lot of parties to go to during Christmas season and I feel I owe it

to them after my kitchen fiasco.

   Last week, after loading the dishwasher, I put Joy liquid soap in, and started the machine on the heavy cycle. Later, I heard a commotion in the kitchen. I went downstairs, and there was Mrs. Malloy, red-faced, looking at this frothing giant spewing cascades of bubbles on to the carpet. When I asked what happened, she picked up the green detergent box and tapped on the word "automatic." "It's specially formulated," she said, shaking her head. "You can't use any old detergent." All week she's been gabbing about it on the phone to her friends. I offered to pay for a new carpet although I didn't even know what it would cost. But she calmed down, and had it steam cleaned, and when I apologized again, she said I could make up by teaching Jason to play the guitar. I was delighted with the deal, but Janice sneered and said it was slave labor. Didn't I know what private music lessons cost?

Glancing back, I re-read the letter, crumple it and toss it in the waste paper basket. It's pointless to confide in Ma, or anyone back home, for that matter. We live on different planets now.

My door is ajar and I can hear snippets of Johnny Carson's monologue. The Malloys are laughing softly in their bedroom. Ann Malloy is only eight years older than I, petite, pretty, rich, with three lovely children. And John Malloy, a rugged version of JFK, has a smile to melt granite. How did they find their Camelot? Quietly, I tiptoe to the landing, sit on the step and lean my head against the banister straining to listen. The soft, teasing laughter dies away, changes to whispers and muffled moans in the darkness. I close my eyes and press against the smooth, curving spindles of the stairway. When silence comes, I creep back up to my room. Moonlight is streaming through clusters of red berries in the holly tree outside my window. I fall into my pillow aching. I dream John Malloy and I are eating Muglai chicken and hot, piping wheat *nans* in the Taj Mahal restaurant under a glittering chandelier spewing colored bubbles of soap suds. And when I turn, he kisses my mouth; and his hand is soft like velvet on my thigh, but then I open my eyes and find my bed is empty, my body pressed into the wall.

"You don't know what happy hour is?" Dr. Barrett asks, amazed. "Never been to happy hour with a friend?" I shake my head, no, unsure of what he means, ashamed of my ignorance. "No what? No happy hour or no friends?"

"Both, Sir. There's no time. Mornings, I have classes; afternoons, I do lab work for my stipend." I sound defensive even to my own ears.

I meet him in the faculty parking lot, front row, space number five, reserved for tenured professors only. He says we can drive on Lee Avenue, then turn left on Winding Way, instead of walking across campus. I sit up front in his clean white Pontiac.

"Come closer," he says, touching my arm lightly, "and lock your door."

Our table is at the back of the faculty lounge. The room is like a comfortable library, books along one wall, a few chairs clustered around coffee tables sprinkled with magazines. Except for a young man grading papers behind a Chinese screen, the room is almost empty. I settle in a chair facing a charcoal sketch of the east end of the University campus and spread my books on the table. He sits facing the entrance of the lounge.

"What'll you have?" he asks.

"I don't know," I answer, "I don't drink."

"Don't drink?"

"Just shandy."

"Shandy?"

"Yes, Sir, that's beer mixed with lemonade."

"Ah!" he smiles, bemused. "Then, I know exactly what you'll like."

He returns carrying two wide glasses—one with a clear liquid and an oval green fruit; the other yellow with a cherry, an orange slice poised on the glass rim. He hands me the cherry glass on a white cocktail napkin embossed with the university emblem.

"Cheers," he smiles, taking a formidable sip, smacking his lips. I sip my drink tentatively, and immediately love the taste. "What's this called, Sir?"

"Whisky sour," he says, "and will you please stop calling me Sir?"

"That's what we call our professors in India, Sir. It's a British custom, I guess."

"Well, you're not in India. This is America. Here, open your mouth."

He picks up the cherry by its stalk and dangles it over my open mouth, watching my lips close over the sweet red fruit. I bite tentatively, expecting a seed. I have not tasted a cherry before.

"What's the matter?"

"Don't cherries have seeds, Sir?"

"They do. These are maraschino cherries. They're seedless."

"Oh! What's in the drink, Sir?" I point to my glass.

"Bourbon and lemon juice. You like it, don't you?" He watches my eyes, like a mongoose. "More than—uh—what's the word?"

"Shandy."

"Ah, shandy," he laughs.

"What's your drink called, Sir?"

"Martini."

"What's the green thing with the red top?"

"An olive. Jesus, you don't know what an olive is? Here, open your mouth. Watch out, it's tart, not sweet like the cherry." He picks the olive out with his thumb and fore-finger. I make an O with my mouth; he rests his fingers on my lips, holds the olive in place. I bite down, grimacing. "Warned you," he laughs, then bends over and dabs my lips with the napkin. He drains his glass and goes over to the bar for a refill, chatting amiably with a professor from the Chemistry department. I'd seen him in the science hallways before. They turn, catch my eye, and wave.

After happy hour, Dr. Barrett and I walk out to the parking lot. "I can walk home, Sir," I say. "I live near here."

"Oh, you do? This is quite a ritzy neighborhood," he says, opening the car door. "Hop in; I'll drive you home. You have a lot of books to carry." I climb in. "Where to?" he asks.

"Dogwood Avenue."

The car starts up smoothly and we pull out into the traffic on Winding Way, turn left on Grant past the clock tower, and left again on Dogwood under a canopy of leaf-less trees. Majestic homes with manicured yards line the street. After a wide curve in the road, I point to a brick house with stately white columns nestled behind tall yews. In the front yard, I see James tossing a football to his friend, Stevie.

Dr. Barrett jams on the brakes. "Jesus, you live here? In *this* mansion?"

I nod. "With the Malloys. I work for them, Sir, in exchange for room and board."

"Nice arrangement," he says, turning off the engine. "Well, did you enjoy yourself?"

"I did. Thank you, Sir."

"You like whiskey sours, don't you?"

I smile, nodding. He comes around the side, opens the car door and hands me my stack of books. "Well, we'll do this again, soon."

"Oops!" Jamie yells, as the football comes sailing toward us, and misses Dr. Barrett's car by a hair.

"Oh boy, that was close," Dr. Barrett says, "I'll see you in class, Prem, and then on Tuesday for extra help?" His eyes hold mine for an instant, then he drives away.

James runs forward and Stevie goes after his football. "Hey Prem. Need help?"

I give him a few books to carry. Jamie is my favorite child, almost nine years old, a middle child, not as smart, popular or anything else as his brother and knows it well, from everyone telling him once too many times.

"Who's that man?" he asks, yanking open the screen door. "Your boyfriend?"

The words are shocking, and coming from James, they feel like a slap.

"What? Oh God, no. He's my teacher. Physics teacher," I explain.

James grins sweetly, dimples and freckles merging. "Will you play with me?" He points to Stevie's receding back. "Look, Stevie took his ball and went home."

I set my books on the brick steps next to a pot of dried mums. "Five minutes, Jamie, no more. Hurry and go bring your ball."

Thinking back, I realize now how sex dominated my life as an adolescent, simply by pretending it didn't exist. My mother never talked about it. Not once. Come to think of it, I don't think she ever used that three letter word. In fact, it ranked right up there with all the bad words of our time—bastard, swine, damn fool, stupid ass! But my mother talked about love. Love of God, country, family, people. Love of just about anything except sex. She said the word "love" with a long drawl, ending with her lower lip tucked behind the "v.' "Lu—uv," like that. It sounded sweet, soft, cloying. I guess love, marriage, ands sex were all synonyms, inseparable like the holy trinity. The closest she came to explaining sex was when I turned thirteen, and she suggested I adopt Maria Goretti as my patron saint.

"Why?" I wanted to know.

"Because you don't have a Catholic name, Premila," she said, referring to that denuded bone of contention between my father and herself. My father, a politically astute man, had insisted upon a Hindu name as a verbal disguise for our unfavorable minority status. Just sounding like people in power, he reasoned, might open doors for me. To my mother, it was a betrayal of our faith, jeopardizing my chances of a front seat in the tiers of heaven.

"No, I mean, why Maria Goretti? Why not Saint Philomena or Saint Agnes?"

She didn't answer. That evening, we were sitting in the verandah off the kitchen. The monsoons had broken; the rain falling in sheets of white silk, splattering on the cement, erasing hopscotch lines I'd drawn on the black tar. The guava trees were drooping with fruit, some yellow and ripe, some still green. I could barely hear my mother over the rush of water in the gutter. She was unfolding a newspaper wrapped in a damp plastic bag. Inside the paper, a fish, a foot long, lay glistening, a big glassy eye stuck in his head, staring up at us. Ma lifted him by his tail on to her wooden cutting board, crushed the newspaper and stuffed it back into the plastic bag, then dropped the bag on the cement floor at her feet.

"For a young girl, Maria Goretti is ideal. You know her story, no?"

"She was a martyr," I said.

"Of course," Ma said, impatiently. "But why? Why?"

I didn't know. I watched Ma—the way her index finger was poised on the blunt edge of the knife, the way her bony wrist moved side to side in rapid fire flicking thin scales off. Light-shot and translucent, they lay glittering like tiny prisms; one flew off and landed on her throat dangling like an opal pendant. I stared, my eyes wandering down to where her breasts burst from her blouse, and then down to my tingling, just-forming ones that were barely discernible under my shirt.

"Maria was a young village girl, pretty with long hair—a shepherdess," my mother said, turning the fish over. "She loved the Virgin Mary so dearly that she recited the rosary while tending her sheep."

Fish scales began flying again like transparent mica chips. Later, she would grind them along with eggshells and papaya skin and fertilize the rose bushes.

"But then," my mother's voice rose, "a shepherd boy from the neighboring village fell in love with Maria."

I watched Ma's deft hands, how her knife was poised, the thin curved edge glinting, and ready to slit open the belly of the freshly scaled fish. Suddenly she stopped, looked up; her eyes pinned on mine.

"Finally," she said, "Maria died."

An eternity crowded by time floated by. "Died? How?" I cried, my voice high.

"Because the shepherd boy grabbed her by her hair and stabbed her. Once, twice, thrice," my mother screamed, jabbing the air. "She wouldn't—uh, do what he wanted. She just wouldn't."

I looked down at the cutting board. Ma had sliced and gutted the limpid fish with one curve of her wrist. The slimy insides lay coiled on the cutting board, soft and pinkish green. The fish's eye still shone in its decapitated head.

"But why? Why?" I whispered, tears lurking.

"Because she was pure," my mother said.

Darkness pooled in the clefts of my heart as water collects in wells. What did he want? I watched Ma stuff the fish with masala, a paste of coconut and red chilies in vinegar, and pictured Maria with her beautiful hair lying there. Ma's fingers were blood red; my fingers were cold.

"She wasn't afraid to die. She was a holy girl." My mother's voice sliced my thoughts. She laid the fish carefully in an aluminum pan, piling it high with pungent masala, ready to bake. Except for its bluish tail flecked with black, it was covered in red.

I didn't eat dinner that night. Ma felt my forehead, thought it was warm, made me swallow two crushed aspirin mixed with cane sugar, rubbed my chest with Vicks and sent me off to bed. Under the mosquito net, I lay awake listening to the rain, her words sounding deep in my ears, thinking of villagers huddled in their tarpaulin covered shacks on hill sides, wondering if Maria had lived with her mother. Through the open window, the lusty call of frogs filtered in.

That night, in a curved sleep, I heard the shepherd boy playing his flute under the guava tree. He leaned against the iron gate plucking trumpet shaped honey suckle blossoms, sipping their nectar, one for me, one for him. He wrapped my long hair round his neck and kissed me slowly, sweetly on my eyes, my lips, my neck. The rain had stopped; the sky washed in cinnamon. I wished I could tell Maria how it felt. I was about her age and I couldn't imagine tasting death.

The next day, I adopted Maria as my patron saint. Ma embraced me and signed my forehead with a cross, her eyes shining.

Whenever I go for extra help, I see that Dr. Barrett's desk calendar is marked with many squiggles denoting interviews, meetings, lectures and lunches. But Fridays, after 4 o'clock, is left blank. It is noticeable, that stark whiteness on the pad. And when we walk out together for happy hour, I feel pride.

It is a ritual like Sunday mass at Newman Chapel. We always start with the cherry. He looks intently, his eyes on my face, while I eat it. And sometimes, he gulps his drink faster than I can eat the cherry. This evening, his face is as crimson as the center of the olive. He is on his third drink.

"So, Prem," he says, lifting my left hand to the light. "Let me see your ring."

"It's my grandmother's, Sir."

He peers at five little sapphires. "It's beautiful. You have lovely long fingers. Do you play the piano?"

"No, Sir." I try gently to retrieve my hand. "Couldn't afford it."

He turns my hand palm up and traces the lines slowly, fingers gliding past my wrist toward my elbows and back again. This is no big deal, I think. He is bored because I am stupid.

"Sir," I ask, "how would you calculate the velocity of an object. . ."

"Let's see," he scribbles using his left hand, his right hand still clasping my fingers under the table. This means nothing. I think to myself, feeling the heat of his skin.

After that evening, it becomes routine. He entwines his fingers in mine and places them in my lap in the folds of my sari. That's just how we sit every Friday. Sometimes, he kisses each finger. His lips are light, almost pink and the skin on his hands is translucent, mottled with pigmented blotches like burns that haven't healed. Sometimes, he dips my fingers in his martini, then sucks them, one by one, slowly. I don't look at him while he is doing this, I don't ask him to stop; I don't ask why. All I want is to pass Physics.

I pass the first semester with a low C. But, the course is getting harder, and Dr. Barrett is rushing through the curriculum to compensate for cancelled classes. Ever since Cambodia was invaded, the campus has been restless. Last month, the ROTC building was set on fire. Student rallies were held in the main quad, fliers pasted on walls and pinned to tree trunks. The air is electric as if the monsoons are about to break. I decide I need to keep going for extra help.

The board is always wiped clean when I enter. Dr. Barrett draws two vertical lines dividing the surface into thirds and writes a problem in each section, then sits down and watches. I work at the black board, my back to him. We have a kind of unspoken deal. I must not cover my shoulders with my *sari*; I must let it hang leaving the midsection of my back exposed. I feel his eyes descend from the top of my scalp, past my neck, down each vertebra like rungs on a ladder, lingering on my buttocks, the silhouette of legs under my *sari*, the bottom of my heels. When I struggle with a formula, he jumps up, puts his arm around my waist and takes the chalk from my hand. Once, I asked if I could work in my notebook but he said no, I should redo them later. It would be good practice.

It is a lovely Tuesday in early spring, a fortnight to final exams, and I'm on my way to see Dr. Barrett. I start across campus, playfully counting dogwoods, pink, white, pink, white, as I walk. Suddenly, from the direction of the quad, I hear a faint singsong.

Rhythmic chants, then one lone voice, then a chorus. A nervous, curious feeling grips my stomach. As I round the bend, I see rumbling activity near the north campus gate. Students carrying placards march single file around a life sized statue of George Washington.

"Stop the war, America," a boy with a bullhorn bellows.

"Stop the war, America," they echo back.

"Come home."

"Come home."

Big black letters framed in skulls jab the morning air, up and down. Squatted on the grass beside the pond, a few students hold hands humming, swaying left to right, right to left. Refrains of "Kumbaya," "Where have all the flowers gone," sail on a light breeze. Underneath cherry blossoms, other students read the university bulletin, their heads cradled in laps, some kissing deeply as if to swallow the sorrow that is Vietnam. Campus police, walkietalkies to their mouths, patrol the campus periphery. I quicken my pace. Now I see yellow forsythia blooming like oversized dandelions. My arms are starting to ache. I stop to readjust the weight and when I look up, five boys stand before me. A flash of fear, quick as lightning stabs my body. One boy, the ringleader perhaps, steps forward. His eyes are rimmed red, his matted hair tied with a purple bandanna. Behind him, a boy in a ponytail leans against a tree, smoking.

"Hey baby," he says, "where ya going?"

A shirtless boy with a white peace sign painted on his chest and skulls up his arms swaggers forward. His tattered jeans hang below his naval. He whistles as he looks me over. "Hey, sweet baby Jane." The words are slurred, thick like syrup. His sunken eyes roll like two glass marbles in their sockets. He falls on his knees in front of me.

"It's the Virgin Mary," he laughs.

"Get Joe outta here," the boy in the purple bandanna hisses. "Hey, Bobby. Dave. Hurry." Two boys in torn tie-dye tee shirts move forward.

"Come on man," Dave says, hand outstretched. Sunlight bounces off his POW bracelet. "Get up."

"Jesus, Mary, Peace sister," Joe groans, edging forward. Paisley printed pleats slip past his fingers as he is dragged off behind a tall Japanese yew. I listen to the scraping sound of tennis shoes on gravel.

"Excuse me, please," I say.

"Where ya going? Answer the question, Princess."

"Physics," I whisper, sounding like a frightened animal.

A swell of voices pulse the air. Calling all students, calling all students. Boycott exams. Peace, Peace, Peace. And then a cheer rises up.

"Aw, come on." The guy with the ponytail grinds his cigarette butt into his shoe. "There's no class today."

"I'm going for help." My heart hammers against my ribs.

"No need. No exams. It's over," he says.

"Please." I look past his locked arms.

"Please," he mimics, stepping forward. "What would Gandy say, huh?" He pronounces "Gandhi" like candy.

"What?" I bite my inner lip.

"Gandy," he says, "you know Gandy!" Suddenly, without warning, I laugh. I want to stop but I can't. "What's so funny?" he rasps. "Don't ya care? Americans are dying." His voice kills the laughter in my throat. "This is America. We're dying, bitch, dying like flies."

"Lookie here. Purty hair." The pony-tailed boy takes my braid and swishes it. His fingers touch my neck, glide over my bare midriff.

"Please stop, Sir."

"So what would Gandy say?"

Suddenly, I feel my stifling fear sucked out. Once, when I was eight years old, I saw ten leeches on a snake-bitten boy. The leeches fell off his skin dying, but the boy lived.

"Gaahn- di, Sir, ah-ah, you mean Mahatma Gandhi," I say, softly. "He believed in nonviolence."

And in a flash, I break through the barrier of hands and walk away; wrapping my *sari* around my head and shoulders so not an inch of flesh shows, not even around my ears. I try not to run as I hear catcalls. Just make my feet flow like a river. Like the holy Ganges River in the Himalaya Mountains, cool and clean. I stop inside the courtyard of the Physics building. My cheeks are wet with tears I didn't know I've been crying. Slowly, I climb the stairs past the water fountain. The hallways are empty, classroom doors locked. All except Room 207. From under the doorway, a wedge of light sneaks out. I knock, wait, knock again, sharper with my knuckles, then push the door open.

Dr. Barrett is seated at his desk, fingers laced behind his head. But his back is to the door, chair facing the open window, feet hoisted on the window ledge. He does not turn when I enter. Peace chants float in filling the room. An ice cube melts in a glass of honey colored liquid, an open pint of Jack Daniel's nearby. The rest of the room is the same. Papers and books stacked, the old fashioned blotter, a brass paperweight, the thermometer-pressure gauge wall hanging.

"Sir?" I go to the window. His eyes are closed; sweat beads dense on his forehead. "Professor Barrett, Sir?" I touch his forehead; he opens his eyes briefly.

"Ah! Celina," he says thickly, reaching to take me in his arms. "Celina, you came."

"Sir?" His eyes are blood shot. "It's me, Prem."

"Ah! P-P-Prem," he says, blinking. "Prem." He begins to laugh, a slow gurgling like a sluggish river. "Thought you were Cel-Cel-Cel-i-na."

And now I see the open drawer and Celina smiling from her picture frame, brown hair framing her pretty face, eyes full of life. A yellow piece of paper perforated at the edges flutters near the photograph. I do not read the contents of the telegram. But, slowly, Professor Barrett draws his arms around my waist, puts his head on my breast and begins to cry. And I cry too.

No, Hal Barrett and I never slept together that night or any night. I cannot say why. Maybe, it was that little red dot on the bridge of his nose that reminded me of my father. Maybe it was because I could not stop calling him "Sir." Maybe, I wanted to prove something to Mrs. Jennings. I cannot say why. All I know is it was 1969, my first year in America, and we were at war, lost. Until then, I hadn't seen snow, escalators or soda fountains. Nor tasted a maraschino cherry.

ALMOST A SON

I slapped her face the day she told me she was going to America. She would leave in three weeks. Three weeks notice! That's all the time we had to say goodbye.

"America?" I shouted at her back. "Why in God's name?" My throat felt dry, my eyes stung like I had just made a fresh garlic and chili *masala*. She turned slowly and faced me.

"To study, Ma," she said, then seeing my face, turned away.

"Study more? You've already been to college, though you're a girl!" I said, my voice rising.

I walked to the window where she stood staring at a bloodsucker climbing up the main trunk of the mango tree. Slow and tentative, it's head cocked to one side as if it were eavesdropping, beady eyes alert, it crawled up a few steps at a time and disappeared into the foliage. She opened her mouth to say something, stopped and sucked her lip.

"Who's going to pay?" I asked.

"Ma, I have a travel grant, assistantships. . ."

I didn't understand her babble. "Where will you live?"

She shrugged. "Don't know. I'll see when I get there."

I felt betrayed. All this time she had escaped in the mango tree with the collected works of who-knows-who, gnashing her teeth like a caged Bengal tiger.

"Why didn't you tell me?" I cried. "Who will pay for your brother's college?"

"Ma," she said patiently, swallowing her lies, "I'll send you money. I didn't want you to worry."

For one moment, I wanted to hold her but she had turned back to the window. The bloodsucker was scurrying down, the red pouch on his neck pulsing ominously.

She is tall, toffee brown like her father. Her wide forehead slopes up into a head of straight, black hair. When she was a girl, I braided her hair. Two pigtails, sometimes looped or crossed, like an X. Now she wears one thick braid fashionably to the side and occasionally, a French roll to accentuate her high cheekbones. Me? I'm barely five feet, dark like burnt caramel. My hair, now tinged with silvery curls, hugs my scalp like the Shetland wool cap her father brought me from England. I couldn't wear my curlicue hair any other way, black or silver.

"Cathy, why don't you cut Prem's hair?" my sister Celie asked, running the skimpy strands through her fingers. They slid soft and limp, like over-boiled noodles. "Look at these split ends." She grabbed a tuft and turned Prem's face to the kerosene lamp.

It's true, Celie knew all about high styles and fashion. Me? I was older but not as wise. Until I met Patrick, I had been a postulant in a convent wearing white dresses, navy scarves tied under my chin, black shoes and white socks. Celie had always been showy, like a peacock. She painted her nails and bought glossy magazines with pictures of beautiful girls.

"See this?" She turned to a dog-eared page. "That's how I styled Beth's hair. Isn't it pretty?"

It was. You couldn't deny Beth, her daughter, was awfully pretty, with fluffy, auburn hair cut short with bangs. Her eyes sparkled with her mother's confidence. With Prem, nothing was simple, not even her name. "Premila" is a traditional *Hindu* name, an esoteric blend of love and passion, a disgraceful name for a Catholic family, converted four generations ago by St. Francis Xavier himself.

"It's *pagan*, Catherine," Mama cried in her high-pitched, why-can't-you-do-anything-right- voice. "What will people think? What face will I show the sodality ladies?"

I could see them, blue ribbons on pious shoulders, medals nestled between not-so-firm breasts, sanctimonious faces openly aghast. But Patrick was adamant.

"Name her after saints if you must but we'll call her Premila," he said.

I felt a stab. Was that an old high school sweetheart's name? Finally, I settled on Maria Premila Cecelia. It had a pretty ring to it; I asked Celie to be her godmother, and there for a few years, the monsoons came and went in peace.

As a teenager, Prem was unpretentious, quiet like moss that grew in the shade. She spent her free time in the sprawling old mango tree.

"Don't send her to college," Celie advised. "What good is a degree? Better enroll her in a secretarial course with Beth." That sounded like a good idea to me. Celie smiled. "Then she can join one of those Indo-British firms. An office car, maybe even trips abroad as the general manager's personal assistant," she added.

Celie's mind was like a nice teak bookshelf, big and small

plans arranged by height in order. And Beth dusted everything and put it all in place. But not Prem.

"Please," she begged after completing high school, "give me a chance. I'll pay you back, I promise." Her eyes were luminous, like Mama's when she prayed the rosary at the grotto.

"What if you change your mind?" her father asked.

"I'll stick it out," she replied. "At least I'll have done *something.*"

Like being someone's personal assistant was nothing!

"And if you fall in love?" he pressed on.

"I won't fall in love."

She said it like her heart was a piece of clay she could mold. She convinced her father. And why not? He had always wanted a daughter. I had wanted a son, many sons—for good reason. Girls bring pain even before they're born. My daughters lay so still in my womb; I had no real peace. Wondered if, maybe, they were too still. But, my sons? Ah, I was never lonely with them. With each of my seven children, I could always tell what child I was carrying. And I too had wanted to do it right as Celie had done right. Celie had a son before Beth. That was the order of business, first a son to carry on the family name, then daughters. It didn't much matter how many. But, without the absolute certainty that only a son brings to posterity, there would be no end to longing. I went wrong three times before I got it right with my twin boys. Oh! For that it was worth waiting.

So, even before she was baptized, I realized this girl-child stirred up controversy in our family, and then after all the heartache, she schemed to chase some cockeyed dream, even as Beth grew rich and more beautiful.

I boarded the over-crowded train one rainy night with six young children traveling third class because her father couldn't afford sleeping berths. Celie met the train to help with the luggage and children. She wore a turquoise *sari* with white paisley motifs and a sleeveless *choli*. She hugged me warmly, her sympathy evident in the way she squeezed my hand, lingering.

"You look tired, Cathy," she said.

In the taxicab, she told me Beth was engaged to the regional manager of Tata Steel Industries.

"You must come back next year," she said, her face flushed with happiness. "For the wedding. Beth would absolutely love that."

I smiled and nodded. I knew that was unlikely. No way we could afford trips in such quick succession.

My mother ambushed me as soon as I finished my cup of tea. Her voice was high.

"What's going on? Why are you letting that child go?"

"I'm not letting her," I said, "She's going, that's all."

Mama's lips were clamped in a thin streak, her eyes shining like just-polished marbles. She waited.

"To study," I said, breaking the silence.

"Study what? Can't you stop her, Catherine?" Her tight lips split open like pea pods. "She should've been married. Why did you wait so long?"

Mama was scrutinizing the dorsal fin of a fresh carp she had just bought from the fisher woman. She held the blade of her knife at an angle and deftly took it off, then slit open its belly and began to empty the soft, green innards. Later, she would stuff it with a green paste of coriander and coconut and bake it till it turned gold. For a moment, I watched my mother's skilled hands and forgot about Prem.

"Mama," I said, "You know we tried. Francine and Paul

D'mello brought a proposal. But, she wouldn't listen."

Mama didn't look up. She picked up a coconut and gently cracked the shell with a small hatchet. Sweet, white milk dribbled into a glass. She began to scrape out the white succulent flesh. I gulped, recalling my frustration. I had had such hope! The D'mello alliance was perfect. They were rich. They owned the Ritz Hotel franchise in two major cities, and their oldest son, young Paul, was in search of a wife.

"Someone from a good family, intelligent and attractive," Francine had smiled, sipping her coffee delicately. She was wearing a blue silk sari with a maroon border. From under the pleats, dainty maroon toenails peeped out. I was pleased and flattered. Of course, my daughter was all of those things and more.

"Have another *nankatai*, Francine," I had said, offering my best china plate, the blue one with painted canaries. The *nankatais* had turned out delicious, snow white, moist inside, almost as good as Mama's. Francine extended her right hand. Her claret ruby ring caught the morning sunlight. After biting into the sweet dough, she took a tissue and patted her full lips, smeared with powdered sugar.

"Um, Catherine, these are divine. You must give me the recipe. Perhaps our new baker at the Ritz could try it."

"Yes, of course," I had replied, graciously. After all, we were going to be one family.

"Would Prem be interested?"

It was a polite, rhetorical question. What girl in her right mind could refuse the D'mellos? Patrick sat stoic and quiet.

"Can't predict Prem," he said, puffing on his pipe without flinching. "She has a mind of her own."

Oh! I was embarrassed. I wanted to die right there. What had got into Patrick? Everyone knows money buys a great deal, even a bride. Especially, a bride. The D'mellos were not accustomed to rejections. Paul Sr. coughed ostentatiously and rose to leave. He was really quite handsome in his navy blue suit. Little wonder he was so successful.

"Well," he smiled, "I'm sure you'll convince your daughter." He grasped Patrick's hand in a warm handshake and played his ace. "Oh! And of course, there's no need for dowry."

No dowry? What a blessing, I thought. All I had for Premila was her grandmother's sapphire ring, my wedding jewelry and three silk *saris*. We would have had to borrow money for a dowry.

Now, Mama turned and looked at me, disappointed. "Premila and Paul D'mello?" She threw up her green, *masala*-coated hand in despair. "*Chey!* What were you thinking?" she sniffed. "For Prem, not that kind of boy. Empty head and jingling pockets."

The next day, I saw them together, Mama's crumpled face, her silver bun resting at the nape of her neck, and my daughter's young face, black hair rolled high in a croissant. Both faces were tear-streaked. And I knew my mother had said good-bye and given Prem her blessings. Mama had been right of course. She had warned me all along.

"Watch that girl, Catherine," she would say. "Too much ambition—not good! Snuff it out before she catches fire."

But I didn't know how. I hadn't been to college, not for a day. I hadn't seen the insides of an airplane. I hadn't even seen the southern tip of India, or the northern Himalayas. Suspended here in the middle of this pitiful peninsula, this small pocket of Christendom with nothing but babies to show for an accomplishment! Sometimes, just when I thought the fire was gone, Prem would light up again like those magic birthday candles you see in stores now-a-days. And sometimes, I felt confused. Could I really stop her? Did I truly want to?

Her hair was braided the night she left home. In a pale pink *sari,* she looked almost brittle walking across the tarmac in the moonlight. At the top step, before entering the plane, she turned and waved. I haven't seen her since then. I asked for a photograph when I heard she had cut her hair. Photographs were misleading, she wrote, and when people pose and say "cheese," it is not a true moment. She never sent one.

And now, after six years, she is coming home with an American boyfriend. No, not a boyfriend. He has already given her an engagement ring! Well, I'm thinking, at least he's Catholic. But instead of feeling excited as any mother would, I'm anxious. Agitated. There is always something about this daughter that unnerves me. Waiting for this child now is like waiting for her birth. This daughter who is, after all, so much like a son!

UNDER THE GUL-MOHUR TREE

I am not a woman yet. I know because women have breasts. Pretty women have small, pear shaped ones that rise one span up from their belly buttons. You can see the contours, convex and smooth, the darts pointing taut under their stretched blouses.

"Cheap women have big breasts," my mother says. "Big, like mangoes."

I look at the models in *Eve's Weekly*, how their *sari* borders climb their shoulders. Side ways, you can see a dark spot under the voile or pale silk material. Yet, my mother is wrong, because I remember Joanna's breasts were big and soft like cushions but she wasn't cheap. Savi, her sister, was flat as a *chapati*, and strong like jute string, the kind my mother uses to bundle old newspapers or tie gunnysacks. Once when Savi grabbed my arm, she left a red circular imprint as if a mosquito had danced around it. I showed Joanna the mark. She yelled at Savi real loud, slapped her across her face, then bent down and kissed my arm, and told me not to tell Ma. I didn't.

Savi's face was spiny, like cactus. Her mouth hung lopsided, the way a crooked picture hangs on the wall. I always wanted to reach out and straighten Savi's mouth, especially when she smiled. Or at least when I thought she was smiling. But the most striking feature was her eyes. Her left eye had no black eyeball, just a white glass marble embedded in a socket and her right eyelid was curled up on itself so the pink shiny skin showed underneath. There was no way to tell where they were looking. Joanna was older, shorter, fatter. She had a broad, fleshy face like an overripe cantaloupe, and her hair was twisted in a croissant at the nape of her neck. She wore soft, cotton saris that clung to her legs, and around her neck, a thin, long gold chain with a cross that reached down between her breasts.

Savi's job was to take care of us—feed the boys, walk Veena and me to school, fill hot coals in the iron, pack our tiffin box with fresh rice, fish curry and sweet mango chutney, iron our uniforms, help bathe us. I preferred Joanna but my mother said Joanna must go to the bazaar because she can count money with no mistakes and bargain for fresh *brinjals* and okra which are really expensive, and the woman in the fish stall always throws in a fist full of extra prawns because she and Joanna come from the same fishing village. When Savi cooks, she forgets to add salt or doubles the quantity, and once she left the rice on the fire so long, it crusted hard and brown at the bottom of the vessel. Joanna had to soak it for three days just to loosen it up.

I told Ma that Savi's eyes are plum ugly and scary too, especially in the dark while she lights the lamps but Ma says it's just the way God made her. Of course, Ma brings God into everything. She says the beggar under the tamarind tree outside St. Joseph's Church compound is like Lazarus. God will raise him up and take him straight to heaven like an angel, which isn't fair considering he does nothing but chant all day while people throw fifty *paise* coins and sometimes even rupees into his bowl. Ma believes that God especially loves those deformed people with curved arms who walk about in torn clothes on spindly legs.

Every morning before the sun comes up, I go down to the kitchen in my pajamas to eat the first *chapati*. Joanna sifts a pile of brown wheat flour into a stainless steel pan, makes a well in the center and pours some water in. Slowly, she mixes flour and water with her finger tips and kneads the dough, patting, slapping, thumping like play dough. We laugh at the whacking sound. The multicolored glass bangles on her wrists jingle. Then she breaks off balls of dough and rolls them on a wooden board into perfect equilateral triangles. In the hot, cast iron pan, they pouf up into balloons and the aroma of *ghee* fills the morning air.

"It's hot, don't burn your tongue," she says, handing me a sizzling just-fried *chapati* on a stainless steel plate. She drops a teaspoon full of mixed fruit *Kissan* preserves in the center. I sit on the floor by the back door, dangling my bare feet from the steps, balancing the plate on my knee, smelling *ghee* and firewood, listening to bells tinkle on the necks of grazing cows in the fields nearby.

After a little while, I hear water bubbling like plopping fish. Joanna reaches for a dust cloth made of old sheets, twists it and lifts a heavy vessel of water from the fire with a big heave.

"*Hai Bhagwan!*" she mutters to herself, "Oh! Lord!"

When the water cools, she strains it over fine muslin into cool terra-cotta pots and sets a clean, long-handled scoop nearby for drinking water. She warms some milk in a saucepan and hands me a cup.

"Hurry up, then go bring me a log of wood from the shed." She points to the fire. "Look, it's about to die."

I gulp the milk and climb down the steps, happy to walk out

into the dawn. I listen to the bulbuls chirp in the tall deodars at the far end of the compound. Joanna's voice crackles above their songs.

"Premila! Come back. Come back at once. Put your shoes on. Where are you going without shoes?"

I yell back. "Tsk, Joanna, I don't know where my shoes are."

"Then put my *chappals* on."

Shaking her sandals off, she bends to straighten the silver baubles on her toe rings. I return obediently and slide my feet into her big, shapeless slippers, then flap my way back down to the shed. The shed is close to the *gul-mohur* tree. In the morning glow, the orange flowers look nearly red. I kick Joanna's sandals off and tiptoe over the strewn flowers picking up a few blossoms. I sit on the steps of the shed and peel back the sensuous soft petals revealing long, pendulous stamens and anthers bursting with yellow flecks of pollen. I touch them gently, my body warm from the stirrings of something strange, wonderful and confusing.

It is time for my bath at sundown. The clouds darken. The wind whips around the palm fronds. Once again, the monsoons will be here, pounding the coast, avenging the summer heat. My mother lights the kerosene lamps early. There is water on a crackling fire, boiling and spluttering, ready to be poured into an aluminum bucket for my bath. Savi sets down my bucket of steamy water. I hear the wind howling in the trees.

"I can bathe by myself. Just leave the lantern where it is."

"No, it's getting late." Her voice is firm. "Your mother wants your hair washed." The lantern casts long, playful shadows on the wall. "It's going to rain," she says. "Listen to that thunder. You'll catch cold." Her bony fingers reach to grip my arm as I slide past the door.

"I'll ask Ma," I call over my shoulder.

The glass eye burns a hole in my retreating back. After a few minutes, I return in partial victory announcing, "Ma says I can bathe myself. You are to help me dry off."

She says nothing. The marble rolls in its bony case, a smile stretches in a crooked line, ear to ear.

I step inside the *mori*, a small square of grouted stones, encircled by a four-inch high stone border, and pull the curtain shut. I inhale. A plume of wood-burned vapor rises from the aluminum pail like incense. The lantern wick flickers outside. I open the tap that juts from a cemented hole in the wall. A thin spray of cold water falls into the bucket making little ripples with nowhere to go. They bump against the wall of the pail and burst. Cautiously, I dip the tips of my fingers into the bucket. A few more dribbles, a few more gurgles and I can shut it off. I don't like tepid water. I like to set myself on fire. I begin to bathe. Slowly, I pour tinpot after tinpot of wonderful steamy water over my head and shoulders. Starting at my forehead, the water curves over my cheeks and neck, falls over my chest and tummy. Another tinpot, just for my legs, another down my back. The aroma of smoky water and lye fills my nostrils. Warm and tingling, I step out of the *mori* feeling like a fresh baked loaf of bread.

Savi stands ready for me. She bundles my long hair in a towel, turban-style, and drapes another around my shoulders. I walk over to the bed; she sets the lantern nearby on the night stand. She undoes the turban and gently rubs the towel over my body. The rain is coming down in torrents now; I can hear it beating on the corrugated eaves. A cool wind whistles through a chink in the jalousie.

"Savi, where are my *chuddi* and petticoat?"

"Right here," she says, setting my underwear near the edge of the bed.

"And the talcum powder?"

"Here." She twists the cap to display little perforations in the tin.

I let the towel slide while she dusts talc on my shoulders. A lovely jasmine fragrance fills the air. I stand still with my legs pressed together. Suddenly, the crooked smile crawls out from behind her ears like a snake and wraps around her closed lips. The marble rolls in her head, lands eye-level on my chest. Quickly, her fingers dart from her hand like a lizard's tongue and pinch me where the beginnings of little protrusions are starting to show, pink and brown, still warm from the steam.

"*Aiy, Aiy*, what's this, hah?"

Swiftly, the palms of her hand cup both my just-forming breasts and her fingers squeeze the nipples.

"Chee, chee, chee! Look at this!"

She squeezes harder. The snake raises his head and slips into her ears. Lips crack open; a set of yellowish uneven teeth sneer in silent laughter.

It is a flash! I stand on one foot, pick up the other and kick as hard as I can, aiming straight for the middle of her stomach, quickly, twice in succession. The towel slides to the floor.

"Get out," I say coldly, very softly. "Get out, *now*."

The laugh falls dead, right there on the spot, throbbing and flaying beside my towel. Her hands drop from my chest and find the curve in her belly. She lets out a scream of pain and, clutching her stomach, runs from the room. I pick up my towel and cover myself. I am suddenly very cold, trembling with rage. My small, just-forming breasts tingle from the pinch.

I don't hear the cries, the lies, the story. I don't even hear my mother enter the room. In one swift motion, she rips away the towel. I stand naked. My mother's face, always so gentle, like an

African Madonna, is contorted. With evangelical strength, she grips my shoulders, pins me down on the bed and slaps me hard, thrice, on my thighs and buttocks.

"Don't you ever ill-treat the servants," she says, in cold fury. "The poor belong to God."

Then she turns and leaves the room. I hear her slippers flapping against her heels, loud, then softly fading away. I look up and see Savi's eyes in the doorway from behind the drapes. I stare back boldly till the eyes roll away. Then, slowly, I get dressed.

I never told my mother or Joanna what happened that day. They never asked. Shortly thereafter, Joanna and Savi left our home and went to work in another town. Joanna never said good-bye, that's what I remember, and I stopped sitting under the *gul-mohur* tree at dawn.

LILACS

I always brought you flowers—lilacs and lady lace. Every morning, I dressed quickly in my school uniform, a navy blue pleated skirt, a crisp white blouse, red tie, shining black shoes. I braided my hair in pigtails, tied with ribbon the same shade of red as my tie. My mother waved good-bye from the verandah.

"Hurry," she called, "you'll be late."

I turned the corner by the culvert, and walked until she receded in the distance and I was out of her sight. Then I set down my book bag on the gravel by the roadside and carefully crossed the shallow stream, stepping on smooth, flat stones to keep my shoes dry. I climbed a few feet up the gently sloping hillside and stopped where the flowers were profuse and dense. Grass tickled my shins, yellow pollen flecks dusted my socks as my fingernails twisted the stems this way and that till they broke, stringy and pithy in my wet palm. When I had gathered a handful, I scrambled back, picked up my bag and ran until I reached the school gate just in time to hear the first bell clang.

You looked up when I entered the room, my black braids swinging side to side, clutching my bouquet, while other students unzipped their bags, got their readers out, flipped pages, dropped pencils or passed quick notes under desks. As you took the flowers, your fingers lightly touched my hand; that's when I felt their warmth ripple up my arm, over my cheeks and lips, like a string of firecrackers ignited at *Divali*.

You never asked me why I was late nor told my mother about my habitual tardiness. It was our secret. You waited for my flowers; I waited for that one moment when you took them, your eyes never leaving my face. You put them in a beaker of water, tossing yesterday's blossoms in the wastebasket at your feet.

"Thank you, Premila," your words so soft only I could hear. Then I turned to my desk, pretending that you had said, "I love you, Premila," because that's what I saw in your eyes, and although I was only fourteen, it is still the sweetest love I've known.

The following year, my father was promoted and transferred to another town. The college peons padded up the furniture with straw and jute, creating funny monsters they imprisoned in sacks in big wooden crates. Hammers pounded all day. Slowly, the house emptied itself like a sluggish river into an estuary of steel trunks, crates and cartons.

On the last day of school, I didn't cross the stream. I stood by the roadside in the drizzling rain and watched the flowers blowing in the breeze until the petals were drenched. Then, I walked quietly into class, my hair damp, my hands empty, and took my seat in the third row. You were reading Robert Frost out loud; you did not look up at me.

The Rajah Express to Delhi was delayed. The swelling monsoons had flooded the Ganges plains. The railway station overflowed with college staff making *salaams*, clasping my father's hand, piling garlands of marigold around his neck until his shoulders were heavy with orange blossoms. My mother stood nearby, a string of jasmine around her neck, a baby in her arms and another at her knees, clutching her *sari*.

"Thank you, *Sahib*."

"God be with you, *Sahib*."

"By God's grace, we'll meet again, *Sahib*."

A train whistle pierced the air. Red turbaned *coolies* shouted and waved passengers away from the edge of the platform. The Express chugged in and lumbered to a standstill. Great puffs of black smoke spewed from the coal engine. People poured from compartments like bees from a giant beehive clutching babies and bags. I stood aside, alone, away from my family. And suddenly, the fragrance of lilacs filled the air. I turned, and there you stood in your hand loom shirt, the collar open, your neck warm, eyes flaming, arms overflowing with lavender, pendulous blossoms. You put the flowers in my arms. Then, you lifted my face and brushed your lips against my cheek, against the corner of my mouth.

"Good bye, Premila," you said, and again I heard what you meant to say.

I was eighteen, in college, when my mother wrote you left St. Stephen's to join the seminary. She said she always knew you had a higher calling.

"God chose him to be a missionary," I read.

That evening, I filled my tiny apartment with flowers. Outside my window, a silver scythe brooded in a dark sky, and a lone branch of mimosa tapped moodily against the pane. A light rain began to fall. The lilacs wilted and dried in the darkness of your cassock.

I was twenty-four, and living in California when Mother wrote that you married a former student, my classmate Rose

D'cruz, ten years younger than you, as I had been.

I read her neat, leftward slanted handwriting. "An arranged marriage between two good families."

Rose was slender and dark, like a flamenco dancer, she said. I closed my eyes, tried to picture her. Was she the one with short, brown hair, freckled nose, long legs, and placed first in long jump, that year I brought you flowers? Did she sit in the third row near the window by the world map? Was she the girl whose still-life painting of lilacs hung in your classroom? Rose had resisted marriage, rejected every proposal brought by aspiring hopefuls, and disgraced her family's name. You did the same when you deserted the priesthood. How did it feel to redeem each other in a banal act of marriage?

I knew even then, intuitively, as only a lover would. It wasn't too long before Rose was seen with another man at the *Divali* fair, and people fell to whispering and gossiping like old church ladies. When she eloped, she took away your daughter and a piece of your heart. Old Mrs. Merchant who still lives on Nehru road and knows everything about everybody, swears they live in California. No one else is certain, because you won't speak about it. You won't speak at all.

Now, many years later, Mother writes that you live alone in a small brick cottage near the cricket field where cows still loll and chew their cud, and gypsies pitch their tents by the light of street lamps. You planted clumps of plantain trees in the back; you grow the prettiest flowers this side of the Ganges.

My daughter turns fourteen this year. She rushes down the brick path, clutching her brown lunch bag in one hand, a hairbrush in the other, an unzipped, overstuffed book bag slung over her shoulder, one shoelace untied. Yet, she stops to gather flowers. A sprig of magnolia, azalea, irises in spring, chrysanthemums in fall—whatever she finds in the yard. This morning, she sets her hairbrush down on the broken brick step and hurries along the circular flowerbed, plucking pink hyacinths from the periphery. She wipes the pith from her fingers with a Kleenex.

"Hurry," I call, "what are you doing?"

She doesn't answer. I start up the car. "You'll be late for school. The traffic on the expressway is…"

She rolls her eyes, exasperated. "I'm picking flowers, Mom. I'll be there in a minute."

I pop open the trunk, her book bag falls in with a thud. She climbs in the front seat, sighs, slams the car door shut. The fragrance of hyacinths overpowers the gasoline.

"For whom?" I ask, stepping on the accelerator.

"Umm," she stumbles, "They're for Mrs. Taylor, my homeroom teacher. She's so nice."

I leave work a little early, drive to her school in the late afternoon and pull into a "no parking" zone. On the radio, I hear the Indian Railways are on strike today. The train stations are silent abandoned shells of concrete. No chugging engines, black skies, piercing whistles. No coolies chewing red betel nut balancing luggage on their heads. The railway tracks glisten in the rain and disappear around the bend.

I close my eyes and wait in the car.

The school door swings open and a bevy of girls stream out, giggling. A few gather under a cherry blossom tree to share a pack of gum. Others walk slowly up the hill toward waiting cars. My daughter is the last to emerge. She walks alone pensively, kicking a pebble with the tip of her shoe; that's when I see Mr. Gigot, her young French teacher, walking briskly to his car, a bunch of pink hyacinths in his hand.

PINK FLAMINGO

She arrives at the funeral wearing pink—pink dress, pink lips, pink toe nails. In a room filled with dozens of aunts, uncles, cousins twice removed, all shrouded in grays and blacks like arctic penguins, she flies in—a pink flamingo from Disneyland, smiling and nodding as if this is her party. And there he lies in the same pinstriped, smoky gray suit he wore to her wedding. His silver hair is combed back, every strand in place, thin spots strategically covered. The suit is still new; this is only the second time he's wearing it.

"Why waste a perfectly good suit on a corpse?" he'd have said.

Earlier, I had pressed it and emptied flecks of tobacco from his pockets. Inhaling the aroma, I'd pictured him standing there, packing a pipe, blowing blue smoke rings, the hollow in his neck deepening with each breath. In the kitchen my sons were gulping tea, waiting to go to the morgue, where they'd clean and dress him, and bring him home to be laid out in the living room. We have no funeral homes here as they do in that land of milk and honey where *she* lives. Here, we must do everything ourselves.

She sits beside him staring — his eyes deep in slumber, lips pursed in a small smile as if they share a secret. His skin looks warm, pulsing with blood, not sallow and cold. I have an incredible urge to awaken him, tell him to stop pretending.

"This is a sick joke," I'll say. "Enough already."

But the ivory figure of Christ hoisted on a dark cross near his head is daunting, the tall flickering candles clearly out of place. He was not a religious man. Even now, I see myself gathering our children, all six of them, for the evening rosary. The children scurried, propping cushions against chairs, walls, at the foot of the bed—anything for comfort. I knelt on the cold floor in the center of the room, looking straight ahead, pretending not to wait for him to join us.

"Our Father who art in Heaven," I'd say, louder than necessary.

Sometimes, he came as late as the fifth mystery. I'd hear him fold the *Times of India*, uncross his long legs, heave out of the easy chair, shuffle his slippers. Sometimes, he didn't show at all. On Sundays, the boys rode their bikes, carrying sisters perched sideways on backseats, and we boarded the *tonga*—she and her father with their backs to the horse, I on the seat opposite. Then too, she wore pink! Light pinks, dark pinks, pink motifs, pink *sari* borders. I listened to the click-clack of the horse's hoofs on tar, watched the boys pedal furiously and race the horse, then wait under a canopy of tamarind trees for us to catch up so they could race again. And when we got to Church, I'd lead the way up the center aisle to the front row hoping he'd bring up the rear. And what would he do? Sit in the back, or lean against the baptismal font as if it were a bar. During the sermon, I'd spy him from a corner of the stained glass window smoking in the churchyard. So many years, and never once did he kneel in the same pew with us, not even on Christmas day. I never asked why; I was just grateful he came at all.

Now she touches his fingertips, permanently tinted yellow from the hours he spent varnishing and polishing furniture. How he loved the feel of wood; the grain, the light/dark rings that told its age. That's why he would have argued against a teak coffin.

"It needs to breathe," he'd have insisted. "You don't bury wood this beautiful."

"Wrap me in swaddling clothes like baby Jesus, or in a basket like Moses when the time comes," he used to joke. "A man should be comfortable at his own funeral."

And I, his wife of forty-four years, would say what I always say. "What will people say, Patrick? You can't go looking like *that!*"

She'd loved him well, had never stopped trying to please him, even though he was hard on her. He couldn't decide what kind of a father to be. One hot, muggy afternoon, she lay with her sister under the ceiling fan, reading *Femina*, sipping *chai*. Stretching out her long legs, she grabbed her sister's hand. "Feel this," she said, "look how smooth! I finally did it."

"You shaved your legs?" Veena's voice rang with admiration. "Wow!"

And overhearing her, he stormed into the room, newspaper trailing. "What do you think you're doing?" he bellowed, "spoiling your sister with fancy ideas." She looked up startled. He glared back angrily. Veena buried her tearful face in the magazine. But *she* left the room quietly glancing at me, making sure *I* was okay. That's just how she was. Hard as a coconut shell.

That summer she went to her first job interview at the Pediatric Oncology Center. In a pink, chiffon *sari* with lavender paisley motifs, her grandmother's amethyst earrings, and her hair in a French roll, she looked lovely. But when she appeared, an apparition in the doorway, he barked, "Where do you think you're going? To a fashion agency?" His voice was like a knife. "Take that hair down." She stared, saying nothing.

Later I found her in front of the mirror, braiding her hair. Her dark eyes were glistening. I wanted to apologize for her father's harshness, wish her luck, tell her how beautiful she was, no matter what hairstyle.

Instead I said, "Are you ready?"

"Yes," she replied, and walked out the door as if nothing had happened.

And now, what does she do on this day of days? Pulls a chair up close to the coffin and sits there staring at a spot just above his forehead, tearless. Like a pink marble swan on the edge of a pond. Despite a twenty-four hour plane ride, she feels no jet lag. She doesn't participate in family prayers. All she does is look, eyes fixed in a trance.

And I? I am the intruder—even after forty-four years of following him around this peninsula to little towns and big cities, while she soared to far-away continents, the wind beneath her wings, returning briefly in sporadic impulses, leaving again at will. And yet, she claims her last moments with him with an intimacy I never had. And when the funeral is over, she sheds her silence. Brings out her guitar and sits around in her pink outfit strumming, laughing with her siblings and friends.

"What will the neighbors think?" I say, "Calm down."

"Why do you care what they think?" she asks, almost kindly.

Too much like her father. I go inside and lie down, bursting with grief like a ripe cotton pod. Wrenched from my life, severed brutally, I am an old tree stump, while she has burst into flower again.

It is midnight when laughter and sounds of her guitar die away. The party ends; everyone leaves, and from under the mosquito net, I hear the door bolted shut. Lights are turned off one by one, and the house, at last, is deathly still.

It is 3 a.m. when I awake to the sound of measured stealthy footsteps in the yard. Alarmed, I bolt out of bed, and in the darkness make my way to my bedroom window, where as a young bride I had once stood naked in the moonlight waiting for the man, who has now disappeared. Peering, I see her silhouette against the pink bougainvillea. She is standing there, hands outstretched as if to take flight. She turns slowly like a windmill, humming and softly chanting a dirge as if to wake the spirits that will escort her father to the world beyond. And unbeknownst to her, I spread my arms and turn too, slowly, echoing her loss, hoping our circles will intersect.

PEACOCK DANCE

If I'm not careful, it will show—in my veiled eyes, the inflection in my voice, a quarter octave higher on some syllables. So I must consider my options. Should I go? I stare at the familiar stamps on the envelope: two spinning wheels, one lotus flower in bloom. Inside, on onion-skin letter paper, I read her wrenching words strung like polished beads.

"We were girls then, Premila," she writes, "it's been thirty years."

She lumps us together in one generation like fruit on the same vine, pelted by the same number of monsoons every June. As if the fifteen years she has over me are like dust balls you sweep out from under your bed. As if she could erase the difference between us like she does her blackboard. Even now, she wants to forget she was once my English teacher, Miss Rita D'mello.

I know that much of what Rita says isn't written in her letter. She's feeling alone since my mother died. They'd been teaching together almost thirty years since Saint Joseph's School was established in that parched town of skinny buffaloes and mud-caked, thatched huts. Rita wants to clear the air while there's still time, reconnect, converse in sentences that begin with "Remember when…?" She wants to meet Melanie, my twelve-year-old daughter, show her the old railway building that was once my high school and the new additions nestled amongst *gul-mohur* trees. "At dawn, peacocks still come down in flocks and strut about the campus," she says. Industrialization comes slow to small desert towns. We can stay in her lovely bungalow tucked amid *jambool* groves right there on campus. The fruit are deep purple and sweet. Has Melanie tasted a *jambool*? Besides, her house has central air. Not even the Ashoka Hotel that cuts across the cricket field where I once rode my bike, can boast of such amenities; and of course, if we visit after the monsoons when the ruts in dirt roads are filled with pebbles, we could go to the Gir forest on a government-sponsored safari. She'll make arrangements—an air conditioned jeep, a room with a private toilet, refrigerated boiled water. What an experience for Melanie to witness a lion kill in the wild, she writes.

I re-read her letter. It is a tempting proposition, at least for Melanie's sake.

My father used to say that when environmentalists studied the migration patterns of birds by dyeing their beaks with India ink or ringing their feet to mark them, their freedom was forever gone. My mother disagreed. After all, she said, the birds weren't aware of the experiments and it sure beat captivity. My parents shared a lifetime of intrinsic philosophical differences they rarely discussed. My mother never argued beyond a dissenting sentence or two. I watched her face, the way a film fell over her eyes, the way she set her mouth and dropped the subject. She was like the sparrow that lived in the *peepul* tree in our front yard, small, brown, always blending with the scorched foliage, busy nesting, twittering a little here, a little there.

But Rita was exotic like a peacock, the way she stood on her long legs, her skirt pinched at her waist, blouse slightly open at the neck, a medal of her patron saint, edged in gold filigree, nestled in the groove of her clavicles. And because she didn't wear a *sari*, like my mother and all those orthodox women obsessed with worshipping or slaughtering cows, she stood out, her olive skin and brown eyes reflecting her half-English heritage and a passion for her career. But I saw more. Miss D'mello was full, luscious like an open pomegranate, even though she tried to camouflage her latent desires.

When the government, in a sudden change of heart, as governments often do, refused to renew the lease on our school building, Miss D'mello was livid. She had raised funds and begun renovations, and now the government wanted it back for office space. But Miss D'mello was not about to give up. She came over one evening to consult with my father. In a cobalt blue dress flecked with silver stars, her hair tied back in a ponytail, she sat on a wide-backed bamboo chair in the verandah. Behind her, bougainvillea sprays framed the back like a Japanese fan, blood red, and yellow, iridescent in the evening glow. How beautiful she looked, I thought, how like a peacock, ready to dance. But Rita was troubled. She kept leafing through stacks of hole-punched papers with flourishing signatures and red wax seals. Sometimes, her topaz ring caught the light; made tinted dancing stars on the cement. Sometimes, she moved pages to the chair seat, using her silky thigh as a paperweight.

My mother's chair was against the cement wall where species

of variegated ivy grew thick, their leaves etched in startling white. She sat quietly wrapped in a green sari, blending with the scenery, her wedding band speckled with dried dough, remnants of flour she had kneaded that afternoon.

My father reclined in an easy chair, his long legs crossed in front of him. The top hook of his cream Nehru coat was unclasped at the neck though the evening was cool. He watched Rita flip anxiously through her documents, glancing cursorily at my mother every now and then.

I passed Ma's coconut *halwa* around, cut in perfect one-inch squares around, while under the appliqué tea cozy, a pot of Darjeeling was brewing. Then I retreated to the swing on the verandah, tucked my feet under me, nice and warm, and began to rock gently, very gently, so the iron chains wouldn't clink. I sat there for a long time, forgotten by everyone, watching my father watch Miss D'mello with eyes he didn't have for my mother.

They worked way past dusk, drafting letters to the municipality, the department of transportation, the minister of education. My father was an authentic government man. He knew whom to bribe, how to circumvent red tape and negotiate openly for political effects, then discreetly achieve the impossible over bootleg whiskey, while chewing betel nut and joking way into the night.

That evening, my mother served dinner on blue china plates with white damask serviettes. She cooked a *biryani* of long-grained *basmati* and rich mutton gravy. The fragrance of cloves, cinnamon, fried onions in *ghee*, wafted from the kitchen, upstairs through the bougainvillea vines and the pomegranate trees.

"Ah, Cathy," my father said between mouthfuls, "this is perfect."

I sat near my mother eating little, watching my father laugh more than he ate, his face ruddy and so much younger than his fifty years. Rita was laughing too, the little worry lines around her eyes gone, talking, talking and happily eating my mother's *biryani*. I saw one yellow grain of turmeric rice slide from her lips to the medal on her neck. But she hadn't noticed. She was busy savoring my father's witty anecdotal scraps and charming oratory. Dessert was served in rose tinted bowls—mango ice cream topped with pistachio nuts. It was, after all, a celebration; they were sure the school would stay open.

As the evening closed, my mother invited Rita to stay with us. It was too late for her to travel on those lonely country roads. There were few taxis in that old town of camels and gypsies. Just a half dozen yellow, black topped boxes, and they were parked like sleeping crows near the railway station, perhaps to catch a lucky fare or two when the mail train went through at 2 a.m.

But Rita said no, no thanks, really. It was sweet of my mother but she really had to go. Maybe, she'd catch a *tonga* a little ways down the road. My mother said, true, she'd seen them gather there underneath the sprawling *peepul* trees. I had heard them clip-clopping softly on the tar, past my window, slow and dreamlike, occasionally a hushed whip to stir the mare. But my mother, never thinking, always blending, says, "Well, Patrick can walk you to the junction." She turns to my father. "Actually, why not drop her home, Pat?" she asks, "It's safer that way. Then, just turn the *tonga* around and come home."

I had peered all evening like a night owl from my strategic perch on the swing, and then when darkness fell, from a chair in a corner of my father's den. Curled up pretending to read like a bookworm. But now, hearing my mother's suggestion, I jump up.

"I'll go too—for a *tonga* ride," I blurt out, much too loud. "It's such a clear night."

And for the first time, everyone stops and stares at me as if I stood in feathers in a clearing in a field. My father is about to say something; his lips parted with soundless words. Perhaps he would have said, "Oh, all right Prem. Hurry up." Or "No, it's past your bedtime. You have school tomorrow."

I'll never know because my mother's voice is sharp, crackling.

"No, Prem, it's late; go to bed," she snaps, clamping her mouth shut like an oyster.

But it is Rita I'm looking at. She is leaning against the window ledge, framed in a splash of lamplight, her cheeks singed pink. Loose strands from her ponytail make her huge brown eyes with their purposeful intensity even larger. Her right arm rests above her head on the iron window grate, the soft layers of her sleeve flaring open, purse strap curved around her breast, like she is about to spread her wings and dance around and around, the earth around the sun.

I waited that night under the mosquito net, my ears pricked, listening for the distant jingle of *tonga* bells. Waiting for the faint swish of a whip, for the tinkling to come closer and closer and stop by the gate. With my nose pressed into the net, I watched my mother walk through each room of the house deliberately clicking off lights. I saw her silhouette in the porch underneath the stars. She sat quietly in the chair Rita had sat in, her head tilted back, watching Orion draw his bow and aim straight for her heart, and when the moon rose higher in the studded sky, she wiped her tears and came inside.

After that night, I noticed a change in my mother. She began to wear vibrant colors, sapphire blues, emerald greens, turmeric yellows. She painted her toenails and lips. Sometimes, she piled her hair high in a French roll, tucked in a sprig of *gul-mohur* or a budding hibiscus. In her new plumage she glided about like a multicolored swan, and in her eyes I saw a quiet dignity, a sturdy love that drew my father in with the force of some invisible magnetic field.

That summer I graduated, and my brother followed two years later. Over the years I learned about Rita from my mother's rambling letters—her awards and promotions, her commissions to expand St. Joseph's curriculum to neighboring institutions.

When my father died suddenly, some ten years after that night, I flew home for his funeral and returned three days later. My brother and mother selected his coffin, a teak one with brass handles. Dad was dressed in a slate gray Nehru jacket, his large capable hands entwined in black rosary beads. Even in death, he was an imposing man. Rita sent me a card with a quote from Kahlil Gibran:

We were fluttering, wandering, longing creatures a thousand, thousand years before the sea and the wind in the forest gave us words. Now how can we express the ancient of days in us with only the sounds of our yesterdays?

But it was after my mother's death last year that Rita wrote, a long heartbroken letter, describing her funeral because I couldn't make it home. They buried her with my father in the same grave, as is our custom to share the land.

Rita knows I'm bringing Melanie to visit my brother's family. They live south in the garden city of Bangalore, that beautiful vestige of England's occupancy, among soothing green coffee plantations, jacaranda trees, and mango groves. Yet Rita invites me to visit her north in that dust bowl of one-humped camels and bony water buffaloes buzzing with flies.

"We were girls then, Premila," she writes, marking the night she danced, masquerading as a peacock.

Rita is nothing like I remember. She looks fragile, her eyes deeper than I imagined, as if she had sunk inside herself. There are varicose veins beneath the pale translucent skin on her legs, and her face, once etched with ambition, is muted, yet beautiful. She has taken Melanie to see her grandmother's old class room; and in the *tonga*, Melanie sat up front holding the reins, making click-click sound like the *tonga-walla*, holding her nose when the mare raised her tail and dumped a load. She has eaten *jambools* and berries served in bowls made from plantain leaves. Rita is charmed; she gave her two boxes of incense sticks, jasmine and gardenia, to take home.

This is our last night in Rita's home. Tomorrow we'll go on the safari, then directly on to Bangalore. The knot in my stomach has been dissolving slowly as I listen to the old clock tower still chiming the hours, the mail train whistling at dawn. In the kitchen, Rita pours boiling water over herbal tea bags. Plumes of steam rise filling the night with cardamom. We sit on bamboo-backed chairs under the stars quietly listening to a giant toad's mating call. Rita's voice is soft.

"Premila," she says, "Your mother was my dearest friend."

In the light of a half moon, I see her eyes filling with tears. She stops, bites her lip.

"Did you?" I whisper. "Did he? Why?" I catch my breath sharply.

"What happened, happened once," she says, her voice barely audible. "We were all so young."

From somewhere, I hear a goatherd's plaintive flute and I feel my heart breaking under the weight of so many half moons. I turn at a shuffle near the door. Melanie stands there in her nightgown rubbing her eyes.

"Mom, will you wake me early tomorrow?" she asks. "Miss D'mello says if you look before dawn, you can see peacocks dancing on the campus lawn."

II

"I CANNOT keep your waves," says the bank to the river.
"Let me keep your footprints in my heart."
-Rabindranath Tagore

REUNION

My father speaks to me as if he *isn't* speaking to me. He begins a sentence, then stops abruptly as if his neuronal circuits have just blown a fuse.

"Vinita," he calls, and stops.

I answer "Ye—es," in a long drawl or sometimes a crisp "What, Dad?" but he remains silent until I stand before him. Now, my mother is cut from a different bolt of cloth. She calls, then immediately begins a monologue as if I am within earshot, and if a train or fire engine screeches by, no matter. Her words splatter like rain on tar roads, and if I yell, "Ma, I can't hear you," she continues an octave higher, and later if I say, "I didn't hear a word," she smiles, undeterred, and starts over.

Like now. Only this time, she's on the phone chattering, ten thousand miles away, and her voice is so faint that I have missed half her tirade. I press the receiver hard into my ear.

"Your father," she booms, suddenly, "wants a reunion."

"A reunion? What's the occasion?" I holler back.

"No occasion. It's been seventeen years." The phone line crackles; her voice fades. I picture my mother carrying on, undaunted.

"Tell your sister, Sheila, and bring the kids—it's a lot of money but. . ."

I tune my mother out noting that she's been babbling for almost ten minutes, that's $40, but with the Asian promotion, it's about $25, thank heavens.

The children charge into the kitchen. Amy trips on the telephone cord and begins to bawl; the receiver thuds on the tile floor, and when I put it to my ear, my mother is gone.

"If you want to make a call, please dial ..," a voice intones. I hang up, deciding not to call back. She cannot dial direct, and booking calls via the operator takes hours, so I know I'm safe.

Despite misgivings, I tell my husband, Joe, about our reunion. We are seated at the kitchen bar, two pieces of steaming lasagna between us. Chris picks at his salad, Amy squats on the floor examining Tupperware containers.

"Round or square?" she asks, holding a bowl in the air.

"Are there any corners?" I ask, gulping lettuce. Amy runs her fingers around the edge and shakes her head, no.

"Then, it's—?" my voice hangs in a question mark.

"Circle of course," her brother grins. Amy begins to cry. Joe pushes his chair and drains his Coke, sucking on the lemon slice.

"Joe, you didn't answer. The kids need passports."

Absently, he turns on the faucet. Water gushes unevenly, spraying his face and shirt. I note for the umpteenth time that the washer needs replacing.

"O.K.," he sighs, "If you think it's safe."

"What's *not* safe? A billion people live there, for God's sake.

71

Children too."

Joe ignores the edge in my voice. "What about vaccinations?"

"I'll call the Embassy," I say, scooping up leftovers.

I call my mother the following week. As usual we have a bad connection. I wonder when India will put that highly publicized satellite in space, so we can talk as normal people do. Here we are nearing the end of 1980, over five years behind schedule with nothing but stalled plans and excuses to show for it.

"Vinita," my mother chatters, "I've started making mango pickle for you. Aunty Pauline gave me Silvie's ration card for extra oil." Her voice drops. "Imagine, she's been using Silvie's quota, but Silvie lives in Kuwait. You remember Silvie?"

"Yes," I reply, dryly.

Undaunted, my mother continues. "She's Aunty Pauline's daughter-in-law, the one who. . . "

My mother thinks it is her God-given duty to keep me informed about relatives as if the trivial details of life stored in chronological sequence in the crevices of my brain can keep me woven into the fabric of our family. As if memory can be saved from disintegration against the ravages of time and distance.

"Ma, you know I can't bring edibles back to the U.S."

"...and so I have plenty of oil. Don't forget. Bring raisins and nuts."

"OK," I sigh, my eye on the microwave clock. "We arrive February 6, Air India Flight 105." The phone crackles, then screeches. "Wait, wait, Vinita," my mother screeches an octave higher. "Your father wants to talk to you."

I stop short. My father dislikes phones for the same reason he hates confessing his sins behind a metal screen. If he can't see the person he's addressing, he doesn't speak.

Another crackling minute, another $1.47.

"Vinita?" I hear a dry, rasping cough. "When are you coming home?"

"Didn't Mom tell you?" I ask, cheerfully, above a high-pitched beep. "February 6th, Dad."

There is a brief silence. My father swallows phlegm. "Oh!" he says, "So late?"

And then silence.

I am deep in dream. In my dream, I sit cross-legged like a Buddha on the wings of an eagle flying past salmon colored tinted clouds. The bird's feathers are light and airy; the wind lifts us high as she strokes upward, then downward, tilting and straightening, her strong breast muscles gliding forward into the sky. Leaning as far over as I can, I call to Amy and Chris who are down below, waving, mouthing words I cannot hear. I want the bird to alight, but suddenly, she flaps her wings, dips and then soars. My stomach lurches, eyes flicker open.

"Indian or continental?" a woman in a cream and crimson *sari* asks, pencil poised over a pad. She is standing in the aisle of a Boeing 707.

"Nothing, thank you," I mumble, staring at her silver filigree brooch.

"Nothing? Something to drink then?"

"Just a coke and some Tylenol, please."

"And you, Sir? Indian or continental?" she smiles, turning to the person near me.

I turn too, expecting the children—and then I remember. They're not with me. I left them at home in Baltimore, and I left Sheila in New York, and today isn't February 6.

The bedside phone is on Joe's side. Its ring made him groan. He turned over while I sat upright and shook him. Joe always sleeps like a leghorn, one leg tucked under himself, head buried under a fluff of pillows. Leaning over his chest to share the receiver, I heard a thick Indian accent, the operator's, then crackles and a faint mumbling above a loud hum. A lousy connection again. The digital clock on the nightstand read 4:17.

"Hmm, yes, hmm. Yes, yes," Joe mumbled, striving to hear. His face was a half-lit pensive silhouette as he hung up and switched on the light.

"That was your brother, Sunil." He hesitated. "Your father just died."

"Died?"

"A heart attack," he said quietly, "near as I could make out. They wanted to know if you'd go home, whether to keep the body…"

"Of course, I'm not going home. What's the point?"

Joe ignored the question. He picked up the phone. "I'll call Sheila. I think both of you should go."

"Damn him, Joe," I hissed. "He did this to spite me. Couldn't he damn well wait? Two weeks? "

"Honey, stop wasting time," Joe said, "Come on, you'll need a visa. You must get to New York, so you can fly out to India tonight."

I rushed to the attic to raid my "Aladdin's cave" for stuff I buy on sale and hoard to send home—eye shadow, socks, rubber spatulas, Ziploc bags, instant soups, Swiss Miss with marshmallows. Frantically, I gathered shorts, tee shirts, tennis shoes, puzzles— anything Chris had outgrown that Sunil's son might use.

As the Embassy door opened, Sheila and I were up front, clutching forms and photographs, profile view and right ear exposed, as per instructions. That evening we were at Kennedy airport, but TWA and British Airways were oversold, and Air India put us on standby.

"Please, sir," I pleaded to an official strutting by. "Is there a cancellation? We must get to a funeral."

The man nodded absently and elbowed past jostling passengers. The small waiting area was crammed with squirming babies, creased, watery-eyed grandmothers chewing betel nut, irate mothers wiping snot off whimpering faces. Older children crunched salt and vinegar potato chips, slurping and spilling coke. Everywhere people balanced precariously on the edge of bulging suitcases, fumbling for papers and passports, arguing over excess baggage, window seats, the line moving inch by inch like a lethargic centipede. The air smelled stale. I turned to Sheila.

"Look, we can't stand here forever. Let's get in line."

"No." She pointed to a sign overhead. "See? Ticketed passengers only."

The official reappeared. "Quick," I whispered, "produce some tears. Show grief."

"Oh God," Sheila's voice broke as she fumbled for a Kleenex. "Our father died. We must go home." Her eyes glittered. "Please Sir."

"All tickets sold, Madam," he replied.

Sheila let a big sob escape, almost fake, but it worked.

"Wait here," he said, evidently moved, disappearing behind closed doors.

The clock above the counter read 8:05. The crowd had thinned out. A few stragglers drifted into the twilight.

"One seat," the man yelled, one finger in the air. "Only one, please."

"One?" I choked.

"Best I can do. It's a crew seat," he shouted, annoyed at my lack of appreciation. "Hurry Madam, please."

I turned to Sheila. "You go," she said, quickly.

I wanted to resist, be generous with my younger sister, but for the first time, my heart flared with a searing pain.

"Go on," she pushed me gently. "I'll come tomorrow."

But now high above the Alps, I wonder if Sheila will be home in time.

We are lying on a cool tile floor, the curtain fluttering to the hum of the ceiling fan. My father lies on his back in his vest and shorts, fingers cradling a corncob pipe, blowing blue smoke rings. The air is thick and salty. Spicules of afternoon sunlight dance through the window flecking the sun-bleached floor. A few feet away, Sheila and I lounge on pillows, chewing gum, playing snakes and ladders; the only sounds are a pair of dice rolling on the cardboard and the click-click of men marching laterally across the board.

"Whee," Sheila giggles, as she lands on a ladder and climbs to the top.

I grab the dice and roll. Suddenly, we hear a soft thud. My father is up in a flash, smoothing down his vest.

"Quick. Vinita, bring water," he calls, sharply.

Over in the corner, he bends and picks up a sparrow, flayed by the blades of the churning fan as she flew in through the open window. Quickly, my father carries her in the palm of his hand into his study and sets her trembling brown-flecked body on his glass-topped table. Adjusting his specs, he drizzles water into her beak with an eyedropper. She lies motionless. With the tip of his finger, he strokes the crest of her head, but her eyelids stay closed. From a tray of assorted instruments, he selects a blunt forceps and gently lifts her ripped wing. It hangs like ribbons.

"Dad, Dad, is she dead?" I stare into my father's face.

"No, but she will be," he hesitates. "Unless I amputate her wing."

"Then, hurry," I urge. "Hurry, Dad. I don't want her to die."

My father looks at me, sadly. "But without a wing, would she want to live?" he asks.

The plane circles twinkling lights. Down below, Bombay's harbor is dotted with ships. The intercom crackles; a crisp, plastic voice begins, "*Namaste*, ladies and gentlemen. We are approaching ...." Dabbing my face with a wet wipe, I buckle up and close my eyes, swallow bile and prepare to land.

My brother Sunil walks toward me, his face drawn like crumpled leather.

"Why'd you come? I'd have taken a cab. You have so much to do," I chatter, hugging him tight, not stopping. "How's Mom? How are your kids? Imagine, the flight was sold out; I came on a crew seat. Sheila is still in New York. She'll be here tomorrow; you know there's only one flight each day..."

Leading me to a wooden bench near the luggage carousel, my brother puts an arm around me. "Vinita," his voice is soft. "Sit down."

"What's the matter? You look terrible. I bet you didn't sleep one bit, and. . ."

"Vinita, listen to me. It was a bad phone connection," my brother says.

My heart lurches. "What connection?"

"Joe misunderstood. He called us after you left Baltimore but he couldn't reach you in New York. It was too late. . ."

"Late for what?" I ask, baffled.

Sunil gathers me in his arms. "It isn't Dad," he says, his voice breaking. I press my face into his shoulder, not wanting to listen. "It's—it's Ma," he whispers, "She's gone."

77

I close my eyes and cling to my brother. There is so much to find out; but for now, I listen only to his beating heart, and mine.

LADY IN WHITE

My mother saw her two years before I did. I remember; we lived in that old, white, cinder block house at the bottom of the hill, the one with cow-dung floors and climbing roses sprawled over the scabby painted porch. Rough-hewn stone steps dipped into a backyard carpeted with luscious, half-eaten mulberries, while overhead, mynas and sparrows melted through the trees crushing purple fruit. Just beyond, a thin stream dwindled to a trickle where, snuggled under tall fronds, clumps of plantains no bigger than my thumb, were forming. But strange circumstances drove us away before the plantains ripened.

"Remember that abandoned cricket field behind the church cemetery?" my mother recalled years later. "Well, one sultry Good Friday evening, Dad and I were returning home after the Stations of the Cross. Dad's flashlight beamed straight ahead like a yellow cone of fireflies, and I walked alongside him. The air felt heavy like sodden cloth. If only the monsoons would break early this year, I thought moodily, and as if in answer, the wind picked up and clouds began to gather overhead. Without speaking, we quickened our pace, keeping time to the croaking frogs and rasping crickets. Suddenly, the air chilled, as if we had stepped inside an icy cloud. Just ahead, was the silhouette of a woman draped in a white, filmy *sari*. Dad must have felt something ominous too because his flashlight wavered. Intuitively he stepped closer to me. I squinted, wondering from where the lady had appeared. There were no houses or trees in view, just short cropped patches of dry grass craving the blessings of rain, and nothing else, nothing before or behind us. The land was as flat as a *chapati*. Behind us, someone had left a cricket bat against a moldy, sunken wicket stump among tufts of ragged dandelions and welts of red clay.

From the corner of my eye, I glimpsed your father's eyes boring into her back as if to ignite her fine, muslin *sari*. My heart thrashed against my ribs like a trapped butterfly, while she glided ahead, above the red mud path, this iridescent woman with no feet, defying the imprint of our own leather soles, so clearly visible in the light of a rising moon. I could not reach for Dad's left hand because it held the flashlight; and if I moved to his right, I'd have to step behind in the darkness or cross out in front of him, intercepting the beam. Still, I had to say something; by now we'd been following her for nearly ten minutes. If we whispered, we could plan a strategy. I moved closer. In a horrifying moment, my arm bumped his elbow and tipped his hand. The clock tower dolefully began to chime ten like a death knell.

'Ravi,' I cried, 'who is she?'

The words, sucked from my chest, spilled into the night. Somewhere in my heart, I must have hoped this was a moonlight illusion. But, when he didn't say, 'Who?' or 'What are you talking about?' my throat turned to sand.

Up ahead, she stopped abruptly, suspended in air, as if she'd heard and wished to answer me. We stood rooted like coconut trees in a monsoon gale. We heard our shoes scraping, braking hard on the mud. The flashlight tipped higher as she pivoted in slow motion, a graceful half turn, her *sari* floating out from under her, dissolving. And when the light beam fell upon her face, there was nothing there. No features. No sad or terrifying eyes, no pencil thin or full lips. Just a blank, translucent oval like a yolk-less egg held up to a light.

We waited, not daring to move, wondering what she had a mind to do. Would she walk toward us with feet she didn't have? On whom would her shadow fall first? Would she squeeze life out one breath at a time or suck it out in one big gulp like the Giant Water bug? The moment stretched, as if she inhaled our terror and would take her time savoring it. At dawn, they'd find us, your father and I, clutched in an embrace, eyes glazed, mouths popped open in two big Os. In bullock carts piled high with jute sacks, the village boys would yank their reins, stop abruptly, jump down and run screaming on spindly legs back toward the main road. Scarred for life, those kids would find another route to the bazaar, bypassing the cricket field from then on.

And that's when it came to me. In a flash, you, *my* child, *my* baby, waiting at home, just below that looming hill. Mohan, our stalwart servant, would have lit the kerosene lamps by now, fed you rice and peas and put your pajamas on, the ones with baby elephants. In that moment, I wanted you with a desire so strong, it seared my heart, and everything I had ever felt, even terror, burned like flaming coals.

Suddenly, I yanked the roots from under my feet and stepped forward in front of your father's ashen face into the yellow beam of light. The world turned black, even the moon's dove gray face faded. The lady looked at me, and I at her, for in the changing light, she had a pair of eyes, cold and clear as shaved ice. She seemed perilously close. If I must die, I thought, this is how I want to die: fighting for love, not cowering in fear.

And then, someone gripped my shoulders so firmly and tenderly; I knew it couldn't be she, for I had felt those hands before, on my face and breasts. My knees buckled, my face froze, and against my neck I felt your father's breath, his whispers, 'Steady Meena, steady.' A light rain began to fall. Without a word, we got back in step. Up ahead, in the distance, the soft glow of the *Petromax* beckoned from our porch. *She was gone.*

What happened next, was even more eerie, my mother remembers. Mohan, a holy man who had spent two years meditating in an ashram by the Narmada river before coming to work for us, rushed to the door, distraught. He *knew* something had happened. As always, after feeding and bathing me, he was reading a story out loud when I began to scream uncontrollably. He flipped pages. Had he overlooked a scary picture? Was my stomach griping? Had the peas fermented? He picked me up, but I lurched about in his arms, eyes bulging, my face like a bruise, the color of congealed blood. At that moment, the clock tower chimed ten.

As I clawed him, he rushed into the kitchen, flung open earthen pots of salt and red chilies, and began to perform "*Disht*," an ancient exorcism ritual. Waving fists full of coarse, granular salt and dried chilies, he chanted loudly, then threw the spices on smoldering coals. Fire crackled, pungent smoke burned our eyes. Suddenly, he said, I shivered violently and went limp as a newborn sparrow, then fell into a calm, deep sleep.

To my mother, this story was evidence that love, especially between mothers and daughters, surpasses fear and evil.

82

The lady in white returned when I was six, on All Soul's Day. It was a blustery starless night; the wind sped into the Arabian Sea, wheezing through chinks in the bamboo lattice screen. From where I sat cross-legged on a mat, a book propped against a bolster, I could see coconut fronds swaying like Japanese fans high above the window.

"Mohan?" my mother called. She too had heard the wooden slats on the porch clatter. No answer. "Shut the door," she said. "There's enough fire wood for tomorrow."

I knew it wasn't Mohan. Earlier, I had seen him stack logs under a stone ledge in the kitchen.

"Mohan?" her voice was sickle sharp, "forget the firewood. There's coal in the bin."

She strode into the room, palm cupped over a small kerosene lamp. Glancing quizzically at the door, she pointed at the chipped slats.

"Did you undo that la-a-tch?" Her voice fell away; she stood rooted, hands lifeless at her sides. The lamp crashed to the floor and blew out, shattering the globe.

"My God," she whispered.

There *She* stood in a bright pool of light, a white veil falling softly about her shoulders, arms outstretched like the Virgin Mary, beckoning. Her face was finely chiseled like an alabaster statue, crystal eyes sunk in sockets, and she was smiling as if she alone knew something incomprehensible. The room reeked of eucalyptus.

"Don't move," my mother whispered fiercely, her fingers cold and tight on my arm. I felt her breath rebounding off the cement wall. Reaching inside her bra, she pulled out her scapula, a green felted square imprinted with the Sacred Heart on one side, an embossed dove on the other.

"Leave us," she said, her voice a shaft of ice. "In the name of the Holy Spirit."

Instantly, the pool of light darkened as if someone had turned off a light switch—impossible because in our town, only the streets and public buildings were electrified. A gush of wind flung the door open, and fresh air whipped in, the thick aroma of eucalyptus gone.

"Ah, *Memsahib*, you called?"

Mohan came in softly through the side door carrying two logs and a lantern. Seeing my mother's gray face, he rushed forward.

"What happened?" he asked, "are you hot, *Memsahib*? I'll open the door. Oh," his voice faltered, "it's open already?"

"Close that door," my mother whispered hoarsely. Turning, she gathered me in her arms. "And tomorrow, go buy a brass latch and a double bolt lock."

A wedge of moonlight fell where She had stood. The next morning, the rose bushes were trimmed back and the door soundly secured. My mother hung the key on a nail inside the doorframe. But a few months later, after my sister, Jeevan, was born, we left the plantain trees behind and moved on.

As years passed, I began to doubt my mother's tales, even my personal encounter with the white lady. My mother maintained that love was the strongest of all powers.

Now twenty-six, I am two months pregnant with my first child. I haven't seen my mother in six years, not since I traded in the monsoons for sun-drenched California; nor did I write to her about the baby. I want to spare her the shame, the guilt and gossip, until Eric and I marry, perhaps next year.

"I am so glad you came," Jeevan says, squeezing my hand. "She has asked for you twice."

She gestures toward my mother, who lies bandaged in a hospital bed like a mummy. Intravenous fluids pour into her veins, machines beep in synchrony around her.

"What happened?" I ask, my throat in a strangled knot.

"She was hit by a bus on her way to church," Jeevan says.

I bite the insides of my mouth raw. How often had I begged my mother to hail a cab, not to cross Carmel Road alone? I had even offered to supplement her pension.

Jeevan kisses my cheek, her coal eyes glistening. She looks so much older than twenty. "She loved to walk," she says, softly.

I point at my mother. "How long has she been like this?"

"She seems to drift in and out of a deep, deep sleep," Jeevan says, "like she's fighting it." She bends over my mother tenderly. "She knows you're here."

I pull up a chair and sit at her bedside, unable to speak. When my mother awakens later that night, she is not surprised to see me. Her eyes wash over my face like the incoming tide as I bend to kiss her.

"You-should-have-told-me," she whispers, touching my stomach gently.

"Mom," I gasp, "how do you know?"

"I—know," she says, sadly. "I—know." Tears well in her eyes. "Nimmi," she whispers, "*She*-was-here."

"Who?" I ask.

"The-lady-in-white," she says, in an autumn voice. Her pupils dilate. "You remember? You-do-know-her! But-it-was-never-you-she-wanted. It-was-always-me. It's-me-she-wants."

My heart begins to break. "No, Mom, not if love is stronger," I blurt out, wrapping my arms across her brittle body. She feels like a broken sparrow. Inside my womb, the baby kicks hard, and when I pull away from my mother, the lady in white has come and gone.

THE SARI

❝You're not wearing *that* to John's wedding, are you?" my husband said, as I unwrapped a bundle of *saris* two weeks before the big day. Like a patchwork quilt, I spread them out on the bed—a royal purple with lavender flowers, a flame-red streaked with gold reminiscent of a brilliant sunset, a forest-green sprinkled with amber leaves, and my favorite—my own wedding *sari*, white with a red and silver filigree border.

"Oh, I might," I said, not looking at Phil, "I was thinking about it."

"You're kidding, right? He's my best friend, you know." Absently opening and closing the drawers of our dresser, he muttered, "Where's my black T-shirt?"

"No, I'm not kidding," I said, answering the first question. Phil threw a what-are-you-up-to-now glance in my direction. "You'll be the only one in a *sari*. Won't you feel out of place?"

He had a point. After all, I gave up wearing *saris* several years ago. I'd grown tired of explaining. Too many justifications—no, it wouldn't catch fire, or snag on a loose plank; it didn't get in my way; it took about as long to drape as buttoning down a blouse and skirt. Never mind that millions of women slept in them, wore them to work in rice fields and factories, on construction sites and fishing boats—even spread their legs and popped babies out in them. No explanation sufficed; my Indian clothes were too far-out for a promising career in real estate and our social circle of friends. People wouldn't identify with an Indian woman's "costume," they said. So I'd wrapped my *saris* in sheets like shrouds, along with beaded bags, bangles, sandals, and arrays of paisley *bindis* I would no longer wear on my forehead, and buried them all under my bed.

"You mean *you'll* feel out of place," I said.

"So? That's true. I probably will, and so will you." His voice was confident, without a tremor of doubt. "Ah, here it is," he said, pulling his black T-shirt from the clothes hook on the door. "It's hiding back here. Want to bet Jay borrowed it again?" He stressed the word "borrowed," a slight irritation creeping into his voice. "He has been going out an awful lot. Must be sweet on someone."

"You said he could help himself to your T-shirts," I said, "and at least he hangs them up."

"But it's dirty now, just when I want it," Phil said, holding it up.

"I'll have it washed and ironed by this evening," I said.

When I first saw Phil he was sitting catty corner from me in Calculus 101, looking nothing like the man I hoped to marry. Five seven at best, barely an inch taller than me, slender build like a jockey's, pale skin, small hands, almost dainty feet, a shuffling walk that scuffed his soles and skewed the heels of his shoes. Long, dirty-blond hair, but not long enough for a ponytail. Not my type, not my culture, and I wouldn't have cast a second look had it not been for his beard, and my weakness for bearded men, who I convinced myself must be the most passionate lovers, although I had no evidence for my convictions. He was Omar Sharif in Lawrence of Arabia, Richard Harris in Camelot, Charleston Heston in Ben Hur, characters in my trilogy of the world's hottest lovers. I'd seen each movie at least twice before I'd come to America.

We made love in an empty classroom the last day of our sophomore year in college, and often during that long, sultry summer. Without the encumbrance of family in America, freedom tasted sweeter than my mother's mango chutney. We rented an old beat-up carriage house up in the Adirondacks. He got a job flipping hamburgers at the local Mickey Ds. I worked as a tour guide trekking up and down Robert Frost country—pointing out his log cabin and the roads he took, the local flora and fauna—the poisonous bluebead lily, trillium, wood sorrel, Solomon seal with its red, translucent berries. He brought greasy, leftover French fries and cheeseburgers home for dinner. All of it—the food, flowers, and love—was free. But, even back then, we disagreed about love and marriage, and traditions.

"How can you *arrange* a marriage?" he asked, when I told him my parents had never seen each other till their wedding day. "You must mean *make* arrangements."

"No," I said, "not at all. I mean their parents, my grandparents, *arranged* the whole thing—they conferred with astrologers, matched horoscopes, picked the date, discussed dowry—the whole bit. My parents had to do nothing but show up, basically."

"Whoa! That's wild. Scary. Like a bargain basement sale. Who knows what's in the bin?"

"On the contrary," I said, "it's the opposite. You've got tons of people examining the merchandise at the counter. People who want the best for their children. And it isn't a bargain basement. In fact, it's a specialty store," I said.

"Oh yeah?" he said, grinning. "And how come you're not on the shelf? With a big For-Sale sign on your head? "

"Actually I am," I said. "in India. Even as we speak, my parents. . ."

"The hell you are," he said, pulling me down on his lap. "You're mine, baby."

"I am?" I asked, teasing.

"Yup, bought and paid for in full," he said, his fingers slowly undoing the buttons on my blouse. I could feel my dark nipples hardening under his touch. Then suddenly, he picked me up and stood me in front of him. Taking one end of my *sari*, he slowly began to unwrap the six yards, deliberately, pleat by pleat, his fingers lingering a little below my belly button each time he completed a round. When the *sari* was undone, he knelt and pulled gently on the knot of the skirt into which it had been tucked, and it dropped below my hips to the floor.

"Some package," he said, looking up, his eyes glinting, as I stood there in my underwear, folds of material at my ankles, my blouse open, trembling.

When Phil and I were first married, he liked me in *saris*. It was a good ice-breaker at parties. Our unusual marriage, in itself, was a good conversation starter. "How did you two meet?" his business colleagues wanted to know. Clearly, he was the prince who'd won the princess, and at twenty-four, here in America, it was easy to pretend. Interracial marriages were rare then; words such as "multicultural" and "diversity" were not mainstream vocabulary. It was all very exotic.

In the years that followed, Phil and I tried hard to bridge the culture chasm that seemed to widen between us. New ones kept coming, big cracks in the earth, and too many times I found my shoe stuck, my toes pinched and bruised, as I struggled to keep pace. It wasn't easy. I'll change, I kept telling myself. I'll learn to measure up to Phil and to his family. I'll remember not to wear white after Labor Day, not to walk barefoot to the mail box, to keep my toenails painted, my feet encased in L'eggs, to set the table—salad forks for salads, butter plates, iced tea spoons, water goblets, and wine glasses—everything had a place. I began answering to "Lily" because Lilavati was too difficult to pronounce.

"A mouthful," Phil's mother said, "So many syllables. Lily sounds so pretty. It suits you."

When his family came to dinner, I made beef pot roast, or lamb chops, and ran the kitchen fan on high the night before to rid the house of garlic or turmeric curry smells. I discarded half-burned incense sticks and lit vanilla candles instead. I cooked more than enough to avoid scraping pans, and bought rubber spatulas in all sizes, just in case. If I concentrate, I thought, really put my mind to these issues like a blood hound, sniffing, sniffing, snout to the ground, I'll lift myself out of this hole—my uncouth ways and meager past, out of this frugal mind-set I've been stuck in since I was a child. I would forget those hems my mother took up and let down, socks darned and re-darned, workbooks she insisted that I erase to hand down to my siblings. It was just a matter of time. But, like a recurring dream, I still heard the scrape of spoon against vessel, my mother rinsing it and adding the slightly colored water to already-thinned-out gravy; the smaller and smaller pieces of meat she cut for us, saving the best for my father and none for herself.

It was then that I planned to leave home—long before I knew

how to read about college admissions in glossy brochures. I became what Americans call a nerd, studying greedily, learning the how-to of test taking, applications and scholarships, hounding international agencies, until I found my way to the red, white, and blue, land of milk and honey. Here, I told myself, I'll shed my past like snakeskin.

By the end of the week I still hadn't decided what to wear to John's wedding. "I can't believe you couldn't find anything at Macy's," Phil said. "Did you try Nordstrom's?"

I didn't answer. The truth was I hadn't gone shopping at all. After all this time, I was still insecure about how I looked in western clothes.

"*Saris* are awkward, Lil," Phil said in a soothing voice. "Draws too much attention, especially at a wedding."

"On the contrary," I said, "that's when the wedding party— bride and bridesmaids are center stage. Guests just blend into the woodwork."

"But I'm the best man," Phil said, his voice rising with sensible logic. "I'll be up there making a toast, and you're my *wife*."

"You never said stuff like that about *saris* when we first met," I said. "You thought they were sexy."

"They were," Phil said. "We were young then. Your waist was what? twenty-four inches?"

"Oh, so that's what it is, is it?" I said, my blood starting to boil. "I don't look like a twenty-something, or thirty-something, and so I don't look good in *saris*? I really feel your pain, Phil—stuck with me, while your friends have new and improved models. Is that it?"

"For God's sake," Phil said, "don't get started."

"This is John's third wedding, isn't it?" I said, as if I didn't know. He glanced at me sideways, on guard. "Right on target—

the seven year itch."

"He's my best friend, for God's sake," he said. "You can wish him well, you know. You've known him too. A long time—since we were kids in college, remember?"

"Oh, I remember, all right," I said, "I do. I do wish him well. Why wouldn't I? If it makes him happy; it's his life."

"Exactly," Phil said.

"The only thing is…" I faltered. "I just wish *you* wouldn't wish for what *he* has."

"Here we go again," Phil said, "now what's that supposed to mean? Are we back to talking riddles?"

"No riddles," I said, "it's a dead giveaway, Phil. It's written all over your face. You wish you walked in his shoes. New wife, new home, new beginnings. You're envious, aren't you? You wish you were him." Words gush out like water from a broken dam.

"I told you I'm happy for him. That's it. He's in love; I've never seen him so in love."

"I have," I said, "twice before."

"We've been through this before, Lil," he said. "Every time you get into a bitchy mood…"

"Yeah, it comes up every time your friends dump their wives and begin new romances—the hearts and flowers and big diamonds. You tag along like a little boy. You get off on their excitement because you can't generate any with your own wife."

"Correction," he yelled, "*We* can't generate excitement. We. Not just me. It cuts both ways, Lil."

"My name is Lilavati," I said, my voice breaking, "Not Lil. Not Lily. That's what you used to call me, remember? Is that too many syllables for you too?"

"I thought you *liked* Lily," he said.

"Your mother gave me that name," I cried.

"If you didn't like it, you should have said so," he yelled. "This is a helluva time to dig up old crap."

"I wanted her to like me—love me, like a daughter—like she loves your sister. I wanted so badly to *belong*," I burst out, choking on my words, surprising myself.

He didn't answer. I waited, wanted him to put his arm around me and say she did love me, and he did too, and I did belong, that I was making it all up. But he disappeared into the bathroom and turned on the shower.

Our son, Jay was named Sanjay after my father, who had died while I was pregnant with his first grandson. The name was easy enough to pronounce, two syllables, I thought. Yet somehow, it too got chopped and I still wasn't sure whom to blame. Perhaps it was Sanjay himself, who was the only mixed-race kid in his class. Perhaps it was Phil, who with characteristic humor would call out, "Hey, son, Sun-jay. Is that an echo I hear? Son-sun-get it? Or is it J.J.—" And the two would laugh and get into a wrestling match, a male bonding experience I couldn't share. In any case, since I didn't object, the name Jay caught on, both at home and in school, and stuck. And in time, my father's name, like so many memories, disappeared into a rainbow-colored slurry in the big American melting pot—and no one, it seemed, had noticed or cared.

Phil and I didn't speak much for the next two days. I left early for work both mornings and managed to avoid him the first evening by staying late at the gym. I did an hour on the treadmill, lifted some free weights, then enrolled in *Ai chi*, the mind/body healing class. The second evening, Phil went to Sanjay's school play. It was "opening night" of his performance as the lead in *Romeo and Juliet*. That was my night to lecture on *"The Art of Selling Homes"* at Lincoln College. I had no choice but to see the last show the following weekend.

"Good job, Romeo," Phil joked at dinner. "You and Juliet made quite a handsome pair."

Sanjay shuffled in his chair. "Yeah, thanks Dad," he said. "Can I have some more mashed potatoes?"

"She has a nice accent," Phil said, passing him the platter. "What's her real name?"

"Nirmala Desai," Sanjay said, helping himself to a big dollop of creamy potatoes.

"Oh, Indian?" I asked, perking up. "Juliet, played by an Indian girl?"

"Why not, Mom?" Sanjay said, "what's the big deal?"

"No big deal," I said, covering up. "I'm just surprised, that's all."

"She was born here," Sanjay offered, shoveling mashed potatoes into his mouth. "She's as American as I am."

Phil looked up from his plate and our eyes locked. Sanjay's words hung in the air between us.

"So, then her parents are Indian immigrants?" I asked, unwilling to give up. "Or is she mixed?"

"They're Indian. American citizens, I guess," Sanjay shrugged, working on another mouthful. "I'm not sure. I didn't ask her."

"Will we get to meet her?" Phil asked. "I mean in real life as Nirmala, not Juliet."

"I guess so. I've asked her to Senior Prom," he said, eyes bent over his plate.

I watched him; how he loved mashed potatoes and gravy. And fresh-baked, cinnamon apple pie, I thought. As if he'd read my mind, he smacked his lips. "Super job, Mom. You're the best mashed potato maker in the world."

I smiled. "You were always a sucker for food," I said, "A real BP. Remember what that is?"

"Yup," he grinned. "Bottomless Pit."

"The way to a man's heart," I began, passing him the gravy boat.

He laughed out loud. "Is through his stomach. Yes, I know. You always say that."

"Right on the money," I said.

Phil looked up. For the briefest moment, he looked into my eyes before turning to Sanjay. "Actually, it's not, Romeo. The way to a man's heart is through his eyes. And the eyes are the windows to your soul."

The next day, I left for the mall early. With no appointments at the office, I had plenty of time to browse through department stores. I hoped to latch on to a good sales-person to help me find an outfit. Black heels, with a glittering bauble, might dress up a plainer dress, and a new purse, beaded or with a silver clasp might work. If I was lucky, I'd get it all in one place, but I had to find *something*.

Stepping off the escalator, I noticed a small, new corner store with red sale signs posted on tripods at the entrance. Dozens of multicolored peasant skirts hung from racks; *saris* were displayed in the window, fanned out like peacock tails. Unable to resist, I walked in. The store was long and narrow, the front devoted to clothing, the back to an array of odds and ends—herbal shampoos, carved incense holders, *Ayurvedic* soaps, henna, lacquered boxes, and colored glass bangles thrown in with packets of assorted spices. I sniffed at a green, oblong cake of soap. What on earth was that fragrance? The circuitry in my brain felt disconnected. Inhaling deeply, I closed my eyes. And there I was in pigtails walking home from school under a canopy of trees, picking *gul-mohur* blossoms, or pieces of tamarind to chew on, or jumping up to reach a drooping branch on a *Neem* tree. Crushing the leaves between my fingers, I breathed the beloved fragrance. I'd seen village girls chew on strips of its antiseptic bark, rubbing their teeth with the equivalent of a tooth brush. With a sudden urgency, I rummaged for more cakes of *Neem* soap, but they had sold out.

At Macy's, my eyes popped the instant I saw it. I could hardly believe my luck. There it was, a long lilac dress with a delicately sequined bodice and a slit at the back. There were pretty matching heels and a jeweled hairpin on display.

"It's really very flattering," the sales girl said, as I emerged from the fitting room.

"Yeah, it hides a multitude of sins, doesn't it?" I joked, turning around, side to side, in front of the mirror to check the slit and my hips.

"It does," she replied, sincerely. "I mean, look at the way it's cut." Her hands glided over her hips and lingered. "It's slimming, very chic."

"It's a morning wedding," I said. "How's the color?"

"Beautiful," she said, "brings out your skin tone. And with those shoes…and if you pull your hair back…" Her smile was genuine as she took my credit card. "Enjoy. Have a wonderful time," she said, pulling a plastic bag over the length of the dress.

As I pulled into our garage, I noticed Phil's car was parked. He was home earlier than usual. He'd volunteered to pick up Sanjay's dark blue suit from the cleaners. His black tuxedo with an ice-blue satin cummerbund, the color of the maid of honor's dress, was already hanging in the closet. Phil was standing by the kitchen window, looking out the back at Sanjay's old swing set and a rusted basketball hoop. His hair, slightly long at the back, reminded me of our younger days.

"What's all this stuff?" he asked, watching me juggle packages.

"Guess what?" I said. "I found a nice dress. And some shoes to match. And a hairpin." He helped me with some bags and followed me up the stairs. "The lady showed me how to wear my hair."

"Oh?" Phil said.

And as I pushed open our bedroom door, I saw it hanging there on the bedpost—my white silk *sari* with the red and silver filigree border, a brown laundry tag hanging from the tassels. It looked just as beautiful as it did on my wedding day.

I turned to Phil. "What's this?" I asked, "I just bought a…"

The look in his eyes stopped me. "Wear it, Lil," he said, softly. "I want you to wear it."

I turned away, my heart beating fast, and pulled the lavender dress out from between the tissues. "Look," I said, laying it against the length of my body.

He reached over and took the dress away. "It's beautiful," he said, laying it down on the bed, "but wear it some other time."

And there, for just an instant, the years with all they had held, fell away at our feet like the silk folds of a *sari*.

HALF AND HALF

Once again, before this session is over, I'll think to myself, "I don't care; not really. Not that way." Then, I'll rise laboriously from the couch like a cow with heavy udders, smooth my dress over my rump, squeeze into low pumps and amble out, hoofs scuffing the teal blue nap of his carpet. At the door, he'll say, "Same time next week, Sunanda," in a soft mantra-like voice. He is Dr. Arun Bose, my psychiatrist, with whom I share a cultural heritage—half-and-half, a hybrid, mentally straddling continents.

My first psychiatrist, Edward McKinley, was my husband Rick's classmate in medical school. He specializes in women's problems: mid-life depression, stress, empty nest syndrome, Rick says. His practice rotates around country club wives—golfers, shoppers, fitness addicts—but he's good with all types, even pleasantly plump, career-driven women, and of course, Rick grins, we're guaranteed professional courtesy. The price is right!

Dr. McKinley's office is professionally decorated—striped sofa, burgundy drapes, and a manicured palm at the window, framed laminated certificates covering the wall. He means business; one can tell, by the way he grips your hand and invites you into his office in crisp, metallic tones. He is smartly dressed too—tan slacks, cream shirt open at the collar. But not long after we meet, he begins playing a series of mind games—the "what-would-you-be-if-you-were-a-something?" kind. It's the latest trend in psycho-analysis, I'd read in *Scientific American*.

If my mother were a flower, she'd be a forget-me-not—blue, inconspicuous, shade loving, no fragrance, I tell him. Rick would be a foxglove, tall and spiky with thimble-like, odorless flowers, a potent source of digitalis.

"And what are *you*?" Dr. McKinley wants to know.

"Me? A lotus," I blurt out.

He smiles surreptitiously, as if he has uncovered a deep, dark secret. *Nymphae:* a tropical water lily, buoyant, satin petals unfurling in sunlight. I can see his mind churning, deciphering the significance.

"And your father?" he asks. "What is he?"

"A Venus fly trap," I shoot back.

"Yeah? How so?"

"A carnivorous plant, two hinged blade-leaves that snap shut," I explain. "My father set traps, lured people in, and then ate them."

"I see," he says, sliding back in his chair. "But you still adored him."

"Don't all daughters?" I shrug. "At some level?"

Dr. McKinley thinks he has me figured out, that I resent my mother for desiring a son, and disguising her disappointment at my birth; and so to compensate, I behave like a man. That's why

I am outspoken, competitive, didactic—characteristics so repugnant to Indian womanhood. That's why I am a scientist, tough-minded, aggressive; adroitly blending hypotheses and theories into slurries I pass off as truth. And that's why I don't give a rat's ass about my weight, as most women should, and do, content to hide it under long blouses, or not at all, even enjoying other people's embarrassment and discomfort.

"I'm bigger than St. Pete," I'll whisper, squeezing into airplane window seats and church pews. "I can knock him cold and push open the Golden Gate."

This morning, Dr. McKinley prepares to play another game.

"Sunny," he says, forcing spontaneity, "How about this? Choose an animal. What animal are you?"

Never one to play poker, I answer cautiously. "A mongoose."

"A mongoose? Why?" he asks, hiding his surprise.

"Because I kill king cobras. I am their only natural enemy."

"Oh? And who's the cobra?"

"My father," I say, bristling. "Didn't you guess?"

"Not really," he says, leaning forward, feigning ignorance. "Okay, if your father is a cobra, what's your mother?"

White hail pellets, the size of golf balls, pound my breast squeezing my trachea shut. I have had this answer ready for many years.

"A rat," I whisper, surprised at the gnawing pain even after all this time.

My mother flies from the bathroom, stands barefoot in her slip, eyes dark and wide, clutching a white towel and a new bar of soap. Something soft and furry has scurried over her foot, she tells my father. Jumping, she has knocked over a vial of herbal oil intended for a mas-

sage. Cold water dribbles into an aluminum bucket of steaming water.

"Please Dinesh, please. It won't take long," she pleads. And later, "Did you hear me, Dinesh? Hah? That rat's in the bathroom. Catch it or chase it out. Please." Still later, her voice turns liquid. "Why won't you do it, hah?" She joins the tips of her index finger and thumb. "See, I'm asking for one small thing, one ti-ny, lit-tle favor."

There she stands, waiting, an aging Madonna, begging, pacing her pleas so as not to be intrusive while my father lounges on a divan in white, muslin pajamas, reading a newspaper, answering with silence or strategically timed grunts. There she stands, high color in her cheeks, hair matted and clumped like weeds in a rock garden. I stand behind the door, my eye to the keyhole, heart pounding, waiting. Should I crawl into his lap? Cuddle up and coax him to help her?

Nothing happens. Above her pleas, the wind howls, twisting coconut fronds, the low growl of thunder signaling a new monsoon. I watch her shiver, rub her arms, and hug herself tightly. Damn, I think. Damn. If only I could kill that rat myself! If only she weren't afraid, so damned helpless! Quietly, I tiptoe to bed, climb under the mosquito net and listen. Finally, she shuts the door and goes to bed, without bathing.

And now suddenly, tears squeeze from my eyes, staining the soft, mauve cushion under my head. Dr. McKinley hands me a yellow box of Kleenex.

"Okay Sunny," he says, gently. "Your father is a cobra, your mother is a rat, and you're a mongoose! Cobras swallow rats, and the mongoose kills cobras. Right?"

I shrug in an "I-guess" kind of way. "Well then," he brightens, "the mongoose is obviously an ally of the rat! A friend—a protector, right?"

I turn away, setting my face in stone. "Sunny," he resumes, exasperated, "can we please talk some more? About your parents?"

Adamantly, I shake my head, no. No, not today, not ever, for although he's right, he has entirely missed the point. He is way off on a different track. I had wanted my mother to be a rat so that she'd never experience the terror of rodents again. Members of a species aren't consumed with fear of one another. In fact, species are identified by their natural tendency to mate. If my mother had been a rat, I would never have had to watch her beg or watch my father enjoy her pleas.

I have been crying for two hours straight this Sunday morning. What set me off was my son, Matt's reference to my size. "Big Mama Jumbo," he called me, even as I'm frying eggs, sunny side up, and grating potatoes for hash browns, not to mention scrubbing the sticky kitchen floor earlier that morning. I can still smell ammonia in my pores. Once many moons ago, my skin felt like lanolin, my hair smelt of lilacs.

But that isn't quite the problem. Recently, Matt has been going out every night, pushing the fringes of curfew, while I wait up wearily, peering through rain-streaked windows for headlights to splice the blackness, the hot radiator burning my thighs.

"Put some balance in your life," I tell him. "Remember Karate Kid? One time on, one time off, *hah?*"

I mimic the movie gestures, sanding and painting the fence, a rhythmic, patient, self-discipline. And that's when he slaps his thigh, a hard, slick sound, and grins. "Yeah, right! Balance, huh? Kinda like you? Okay, big Mama Jumbo. I get it!"

It was meant to be funny, not mean. My son isn't that kind of boy, and funny it was, sending his stepfather Rick, into a mirthful guffaw. I should be grateful, I tell myself. After all, what are the statistics on second-time-around families? I butter their muffins, as they talk and bend their robotic arms from plate to lips and back again.

"Cal's my man," Matt says, palms hoisted for a high five. Frivolous laughter rolls like dust motes under the table.

Rick had been Matt's pediatrician, had known him since he was wiped off and measured—7lbs., 2oz, 18 inches long. Shortly thereafter, when he turned the color of turmeric, Rick bandaged his eyes and put him under UV lights every day for a week, pricking his perforated bing-cherry baby heels for bilirubin tests. I would shut my eyes, while holding the screaming, writhing little body, and when it was done, Rick would bring me black coffee and tissues.

Matt was almost nine by the time Rick and I abandoned our stale marriages and turned to each other for comfort. But comfort falls lightly like spring rain, and now nine years later, I find myself adrift on a crystalline floe of Arctic ice, like a solitary bearded seal unable to glide back to sea, or dive to fearless depths.

"For God's sake, Sunny," Rick groans, as I sniffle in the bathroom, "what's wrong *now*? Did you take your Prozac today?" I turn the faucet on full blast. "Go see Ed. Check on the Prozac dose. Get some antioxidants, estrogen, *something*. Anything!"

I meet Dr. Bose in a crowded Asian store one Friday evening. Except for a 5-kilo sack of basmati rice, my groceries are modest—okra, a bottle of mint chutney, some *Neem* products. The man in front carries a basket piled high with lentils, eggplant, fresh papayas. He wears a blue shirt, maroon tie, clearly a professional Mr. Mom who, like me, hasn't started dinner. Up ahead, at the counter, a woman is arguing with Mr. Kapoor.

"Mister, how you can charge for spoilt video, *hah?*" she shouts, brandishing a tape.

"Madam, all sales final. See the notice?" he jabs at block letters behind him.

"But this is defective product, mister," she yells, "at least give discount."

Irritably, I squint at my wristwatch just as the man in front turns. "You're apparently in a hurry," he says, stepping aside. "Would you like to go ahead?"

"No, thanks," I say, embarrassed, "it's okay."

"Go on. You only have a few things," he smiles.

I exchange places. "Thanks."

"You're a pretty big *Neem* fan," he laughs, "soap, toothpaste, deodorant, even cold cream? Which part of India are you from?"

"The part with many *Neem* trees," I quip. "And you?"

"Jaipur," he says, "the city of kings."

The woman up ahead is still adamant about the video.

"Whatever makes people tick?" I mutter, loud enough to be heard.

"Exactly," he grins. "That's what I keep asking myself." He sticks his hand out. "Arun Bose. I'm a psychiatrist."

"Sunanda Rogers," I respond, shaking his hand, but extracting it quickly to make *namaste*. "People call me Sunny."

"You still make *namaste*?" he asks, amused. "That's great. Very ethnic."

"Well, it's fashionable," I say, "Multicultural is in, you know."

"Um, yes," he nods, "but terribly over-rated, even destructive, if carried to extremes. A lot of unhappy, maladjusted people follow this trend."

"Maybe, they're homesick," I suggest. "Maybe they feel guilty living in such opulence—this magical place. Maybe, they're still in love with the past," I add, oddly surprising myself.

"Everyone is," Arun Bose replies, in low cello-like tones. "Nostalgia is a national pastime. People searching for roots, identities, cultures..."

"What's wrong with that?"

"Nothing, except that it consumes the present."

"Isn't that what psychiatrists do—unearth the past?"

"To some extent, yes. But doesn't the past extend beyond childhood, beyond birth?" he asks, softly.

"Excuse me, Madam," Mr. Kapoor interrupts, "if you don't mind, if you want to talk, please step...."

Engrossed in conversation, we had inched to the front. Hurriedly, I empty my basket. "The basmati is on sale, right? $10.99 for five kilos?" I ask Mr. Kapoor. He nods, placated. Arun Bose hands me his business card as I pull out my credit card.

"Perhaps we can talk again," he says.

It isn't until a year has passed, a year with Dr. McKinley, a year of insatiable eating and bone chilling loneliness that I make an appointment with Dr. Bose's secretary.

His office is spacious, serene like a temple. In the entrance hall, an expensive hand-knotted Indian rug displays the story of creation, the tree of life in vibrant colors. In an alcove, there is a framed photograph of the Hindu Trinity: Brahma, Shiva, Vishnu, and beside it, God the Father and a dove hover over a crucified Christ. A long string of gardenia buds is looped around the deities like tinsel on a Christmas pine. Smoke curls from a stick of jasmine incense.

I enter quietly and fill out a medical history form. I do not expect to be remembered, would even prefer it that way, yet near the printed words, "Referring physician," I write, "None. Chance encounter."

"The *Neem* lady," Dr. Bose says, joining his hands in a *namaste*. "How are you?"

"Large," I answer quietly, "as you can see."

His eyes take in the extra forty pounds. "Ah weight," he smiles, "another overrated parameter. Like ethnicity. A national preoccupation."

"Yeah," I say dryly, "Overweight, middle-aged women! A doctor's dream to fat city."

He ignores the sarcasm. "Sunanda," he says, "please sit down."

Over several months, I talk and he listens. I tell him about my life on both continents. He listens attentively like a musician tuning his sitar. He understands why I am a lotus, a mongoose, a career mother, an immigrant—half-and-half, haunted by memory, despising myself for fleeing.

He corrects me. "Not flee. We make choices, Sunanda," he says, almost tenderly.

"Wrong ones," I say.

"Not wrong, just painful," he says.

"Were *you* born here?" I ask.

He laughs. "Gosh, no. Do I look like I'm from here?"

"Well, you don't have an Indian accent," I say.

"Oh, I do, according to most people. You don't hear it because it sounds like yours."

"Well then, *you're* half and half too," I say. "How did you deal with it?"

He rises from his seat and gathers up his papers. "Well, Sunanda, you're not paying me to listen to *my* problems," he says.

I hide my disappointment. "That's true," I say.

"Besides, I'm not sure I've dealt with it, either," he adds.

"Really? Then, will you tell me over coffee? Tomorrow, around this time? I know I'm your last appointment." I see him hesitating, and move quickly toward the door. "There's a place right by the Indian store where we first met. It's called "India

Palace, or something like that."

Arun Bose arrives exactly on time and joins me at the table at which I'm seated. I'm dressed in my jade green and amber *salvar khameez*, a favorite outfit I couldn't get into a year ago. We are the only Indians in a sea of white faces.

I smile as he pulls his chair out and says hello. "I see you don't keep Indian Standard Time," I say, insinuating that Indians are always late for appointments. Back "home" in India, Indian Standard Time refers to a standard of invariable tardiness.

"Ah, that's an in-joke I haven't heard in a while," he grins, and glances at his wrist watch. "And you don't keep IST either."

"No, oh no. Rick's a stickler for time. I had to get out of the IST habit in a big hurry."

We order a *thali* of assorted snacks—*samosas* with tamarind chutney, *kachoris*, potato *tikkis*, and steaming mugs of "Serene Chai."

"Notice how popular Indian cuisine has become?" he asks, glancing at the tables around us.

"Not just Indian cuisine," I say. "It's all things Indian. Yoga and meditations, clothing, and even movies. Have you seen *Monsoon Wedding*?"

"No, I'll pass on it," he says. "I can't stand these so-called adaptations with music and movies, and mental health quick fixes. It's all hocus-pocus. What's *Serene Chai*, anyway? Probably, just some Orange Pekoe, or repackaged Earl Grey. As if you can *drink* in serenity."

I laugh. "Exactly. I went to a yoga class once, and couldn't concentrate one bit. The woman couldn't even pronounce "*Ardha chandrasana*." You know "ardha" means half, and "chandra" is the moon. It was, of course, the half moon pose. The way she pronounced *our* words drove me crazy. I left mid-way, and you should have seen the way she glared at me. She knew I was Indian, and felt threatened, most likely."

"You *are* a bit overwhelming," he says, grinning. "And we're both being overly critical. Condescending, too. There are some excellent yoga teachers around." He pauses, his face quiet. "Everyone hungers for Peace—and Love, words we throw around, never really *getting* it. We search *outside* ourselves. Isn't that what the seven *chakras*, or "energy centers," as it's called here, mean?"

I nod. "You're right. It's all about balance. I'd lecture my son, Matt, about that—as if *I* knew!" I take a deep breath. "I've heard there are places where people, who can't do yoga contortions, go—just to chant. Did you know that?"

He nods. The food arrives and we wait until the waitress leaves. We eat a few morsels in silence, chewing slowly. He sips his water and wipes his mouth with his napkin. "Ah, that feels good."

"So?" I say, a few moments later. "You left me curious the last time we met. You said you hadn't dealt with your own half-and-half-ness. Really?"

"Well, not completely. It raises its cobra head every now and then. But it's easier for me than for you."

"How so?"

"Because I'm married to an Indian woman. I brought her here to this country."

I feel a sharp tug at my heart. I'd assumed he was single because I'd met him in a grocery store. "An arranged marriage, then?" I ask.

"Yes, the traditional way. I went home and met my wife. It wasn't a love marriage like yours," he adds.

I smile. "Love marriages are over-rated too, you know. It's another national pastime." Suddenly, we burst out laughing.

"Good one," he says.

"I've been through two "love" marriages," I say, using my fingers as quotation marks. "I was twenty-two for my first one—to my high school sweetheart. My parents went berserk; he wasn't a Brahmin. You know how that goes. I'm sure they'd have liked to "arrange" my life," I say, using my fingers again, "but in the end, they gave in."

"Then?"

"Then, we came here to the U.S. to get our Ph.D.s and decided to stay on. We got our green cards." I pause, remembering those years. "The only thing worse than *feeling* half and half is to *live* with someone who feels the same." I chuckle, thinking back again. "Yeah, I became the Indian half; he became the American half. Like oil and vinegar, we didn't mix." I laugh out loud at my metaphor. "Eventually, he fell in love with a well-rooted American, who could probably trace her family lineage to the Mayflower."

"Where's he now, your first husband?"

"Out in California. Matt was only nine when he left." I pause, thinking back to the trauma of that time. "He's a senior now. He wants to go to college in California. He has two half siblings, a brother and a sister."

"Hmm," Arun Bose says. "And I know you have no more children."

I laugh. "With Rick? No. Oh, no. We don't have any. And it's just as well. Rick had finished his reproductive phase when we met. He has a kid—George—from his previous marriage." I pause for a moment, remembering. "But he's been a good father to Matt. They get along great. Good buddies."

Arun takes a long drink of lemon water. "And you're lonely?" he asks.

"You could say that, I guess. The older I get, the lonelier I get, or so it seems."

Suddenly, he grins, teasing. "That's not uncommon. That's why they have the AARP. Have you joined?"

I kick him gently under the table. "I'm not *that* old," I say.

He laughs out loud. "A little sensitive, are we?"

"Yeah, I guess. Age! Another national pastime?" We both laugh heartily. "But, more gender specific, don't you think? Men seem to. . ." I say.

"Oh, you'd be surprised. Men don't handle it well, either. They're just as vain, just as worried. The male menopause is a real phenomenon, you know. It's just that men won't acknowledge it."

"And you? You do?"

He smiles. "I have to. I'm the psychiatrist, remember?" He looks at me intently and changes the subject. "There's one more *samosa* left on the plate. Aren't you going to have that?" he asks.

"No, I'm done, thanks. Why don't you finish it?" He plunges his fork into the deep fried dough, happy to oblige. "You like *samosas*, I can tell," I say. "Doesn't your wife make them at home?"

He pauses, wordlessly debating something in his mind. "She's-uh-she used to," he says. "But she's –uh- gone back to India."

"Permanently?" I ask, before I can stop myself.

"Well, no. It wasn't supposed to be. But, she didn't like the States at all. And she was homesick. She went home for a little holiday."

I know I should drop the subject, but I can't. I haven't been so relaxed, so comfortable in my own skin since I can't remember when. I wait, but he doesn't elaborate.

"How long ago?" My voice comes out in a whisper.

His eyes linger on me, warm like an Indian summer. "Almost a year," he says, softly.

HYBRID MOTHER

Last week, out of the blue, my mother has an epiphany. "Viju, let's go to lunch-and get sushi. Good idea, huh?" she says, all in one breath, and although my mouth waters, my antenna is up. What's she got up her sleeve? What does she know this time? Her invitation unnerves me; why sushi and not dosa I wonder? My mother knows I love dosa-those foot-long, golden, lacy crepes, bulging with spicy potato filling. Served with finely ground coconut chutney, it is my favorite Indian snack.

Long before my feet could reach the floor, my mother would take me to a little place tucked in a shopping mall strip for dosa and mango lassi. Cutting up little pieces of potato, she'd wrap fried batter around, spoon chutney over it and feed me, telling me to chew properly. As I grew into a teenager, I declined her invitations, first discreetly ("too much homework"), then blatantly ("hmm, not today, not in the mood"). So, she resorted to carry-out techniques.

"Hey, Viju, you up there?" she'd call, craning her neck up the banister. "Look what I got us."

Drawn by the aroma of coriander and turmeric, I'd dash into the kitchen, pull the dosa from long, cardboard wrappers, sometimes ripping the lacy crepe, slop chutney on, and dash back to my room. She ate alone in the kitchen. In my junior year I stopped eating dosa. Instead, I began dating Steve, and we'd go off to an authentic Chinese place. With chopsticks, he'd pick pink shrimp rolled in sticky rice and seaweed, swirl each morsel in rich, brown soy sauce, and place it on my tongue. Biting into the roll, never taking my eyes off his face, I thought I saw all seven wonders of the world reflected there. Later, at dusk, we'd link arms and walk along the cobbled path around the pond, where one by one, the ducks swam, always to the same spot by the weeping willow and settled down. Like them, I too nestled into Steve's shoulder.

We settle into our booth. My mother is no sushi-eater, so I guess she has something on her mind. A young Chinese girl sets a porcelain teapot with Chinese characters on the lid and handle in front of us. My mother pours green tea.

"So? How's school?" she asks, slurping a mouthful, and before I can answer, she exhales "Ah-Ah" loudly, slouching in the booth as if it's a hot tub. People turn and stare; I duck to adjust my shoe strap and pretend we're unrelated. But, suddenly, stowed away memories of my grandmother unfold. These mannerisms-the way my mother crinkles her nose, uses her index finger to point, slips off her shoes in public, says "hah" and sucks her lip, are direct Mendelian traits she's surely inherited from her mother. Yet, beyond these superficial characteristics she isn't like my grandmother at all. Grammy was whole, intact; her roots were dense, tuberous, like ten-pound taros. My mother is half and half-not a creamy blend, but a split-down-the-middle, bifurcated woman. Her roots are fibrous, stringy, more like a flowering annual that is uprooted and replanted each year. One half lives in America, the other half was left behind half way around the globe. The two halves don't communicate; they co-exist like estranged neighbors, each in her own house, barely nodding to each other as they pick the morning newspaper from their lawns. Both struggle for survival, neither is the fittest.

"Baby, you dreaming, or what? Huh? How's your senior year coming?" she asks. I am tempted to tell her she reminds me of grandmother. But I know she'll deny it vehemently, or give me a long-suffering God-rest-her-soul smile.

"Oh no, I'm not dreaming," I say, swallowing tea. "School is fine."

I'm not sure where we're going with this, but I doubt we're here to discuss school.

"Good, good," she says. She dips a large tempura shrimp in sauce, then puts it down suddenly.

"What's the matter?" I ask, "I mean with the shrimp."

"Oh, nothing, it's the biggest one, see?" She points to it. "I kept it for you."

"Why?"

"Why, what?"

"Why are you keeping it for me? You love shrimp; so can't you just enjoy it, Ma? Can't we order another plate?"

She looks startled. "Huh? Of course, I'm enjoying it," she says. "By seeing you enjoy it."

Ashamed, I grab it by its tail and bite off the whole thing, not stopping for sauce. My mother looks at me, saying nothing. I keep waiting for the shoe to drop, something she's mulled into a large-sized worry, or burning life lesson. But, we finish our meal and leave, all done in an hour, just as I'd wanted.

And inexplicably, I feel cheated.

"So, how was it?" Steve asked, later. "Who won? You both alive?"

"Yeah, we're alive," I said. "Nothing happened."

He mimicked my mother. "Did she slurp her tea, Ah-ah?"

And suddenly, I began to bristle at the implication that my mother, a fuddy-duddy from some uncouth third-world country, had no manners and was unable to comprehend the intricacies of my heart the way he does. Or worse, the way his lawyer-mother understands his sister. Steve has never understood why my mother and I argue about banalities like wasting food; in fact, his athletically built mother habitually leaves food on her plate.

"It's a weight watcher's thing, something about portion control," he'd explained.

My mother always picked at my American father's plate, before rinsing it off. "He leaves half the steak on the bone," she'd complain. True, my father didn't chew on a pork chop or chicken leg; he trimmed pieces off, eating one thing at a time-first meat, then potatoes, then vegetables, often heading for seconds before touching his vegetables, leaving a whole balanced meal for my mother. This, I didn't tell Steve.

Nor did I tell him that my Mom hasn't ever had her nails done. "Too expensive," she insisted. "What they can do, I can do. Thirty dollars to dip fingers in Palmolive?"

"It's not Palmolive," I'd said.

"Yes it is. Says so in the TV commercial."

"TV commercials are all lies, Ma."

"Not always," she said, "you got to pick out truth in everything."

My mother's penury, her inability to let go of her past, is what drives me insane. Even after decades in this land of plenty, she behaves as if she's still in the land that isn't. Innumerable times I've heard her tell stories-of apples that were quartered and shared, gravies diluted to stretch curries, meat morsels halved. I had hoped this living-in-the-past habit would fade like the memory of a bad dream. I'd hoped she'd molt and metamorphose, if not from caterpillar to social butterfly, then at least to moth. But she can't change. Like a fly to fly-paper, she's stuck in her frugal past.

And I feel stuck too.

"Did you tell your mother you'll be real late, tonight?" Steve asks, on our last evening together, before I leave for college. "I hope she doesn't wait up for you."

I roll my eyes. "I hope not. But, she probably will."

"I don't get it," Steve says. "She knows you smoke, and she knows you drink, and she knows you're with me. Does she think you're a virgin?"

Suddenly, my cheeks get hot. "What's it to you, Steve? What difference does it make? Why do you always bring her up?"

"Hey, calm down. I'm just asking. You said she sits on the radiator with her nose pressed to the windowpane." He chuckles. "I can't picture my mother doing that."

"She's different, okay? She doesn't get it. I've told her a million times. I told her American mothers don't wait up all night."

"Yeah? And what did she say?"

"Nothing," I lied.

It is pointless to tell Steve the truth. My mother's answer had been a simple statement. "I'm not an American mother," she'd replied.

On my last morning home, I awaken late and head for the

kitchen. No signs of my mother. I bound back upstairs to her bedroom. No signs of her there, either. The bed is neatly made. In the center are clothes to be packed-stacks of underwear, blouses, pants, sheets, shoes wrapped in newspaper, Tylenol, bandaids, Bacitracin, Cortisone. Off to one side, fat free Nutrigrain, Crystal Light, instant dosa and sambar mix. My heart rustles; where is she? The house is like a morgue.

I walk quietly into the sunroom, wondering, and there she is in a heap on the sofa, one brown hand dangling off the edge, face half-lit by the morning sun. For a split second my heart contracts. What if she's dead; what if I killed her with my thoughts of who she is-a half and half mother? A hybrid?

But then, suddenly she hears my breath and opens her eyes. "Ah, baby, you're awake?" She scrambles up. "It's almost lunchtime. You want dosa?"

I burst out laughing. "Huh? Why you laughing?" she asks, puzzled. "You want me to order sushi?"

"Oh, Mommy," I say, flinging my arms around her, raining little kisses over her face and head, "you're so…"

And I have no more words left, because I haven't called her Mommy for so long, not since I was in middle school when we ate dosa together.

RUNNING

When she looks again, all she sees is a mop of jet-black hair and the calves of his legs pounding red clay on the jogging trail. Rounding the corner, he veers off to the left behind the coconut trees and disappears from view. Surya steps up her gait, arms and feet working in synchrony, her breath coming faster and faster as she nears the lopsided exit sign tacked to the wooden gatepost. Not breaking her stride, she cranes her neck, even throws a backward glance, but he has vanished like some apparition. Forcing herself to concentrate, she continues two more laps before she must return home, shower, and get out again, this time to the bazaar, before the noonday sun scorches the morning away.

The first time they spoke, he yelled, "Your shoelace" as he chugged past in the adjoining lane, and she shouted, "What?" Glancing down she saw it had come undone, a loop dangling dangerously at her instep. Stopping to tie it, she felt blood rush to her cheeks, oddly flattered that he would notice or bother to inform her.

"Double knot it or get Velcro," he called over his shoulder on the next lap, pointing at his *Nikes*.

"What's it to you?" she thought, no longer flattered. As usual he'd gone way ahead again, leaving her with a mental monologue.

This morning he's wearing white shorts with a red T-shirt. On his head there's a Walkman; on his feet, black running shoes, *Adidas*, with a red tongue. She assumes he lives abroad, a "foreign returned" eligible bachelor, thirty something, probably a medical doctor or a promising business executive on the fast track, home on vacation, and much sought after by status–seeking parents of girls eligible for marriage. She knows his type—intelligent, first born, heir apparent, most likely a flamboyant Romeo who enjoys his flings with white-skinned girls, then returns home to choose a bride from a smorgasbord of eager applicants. She envisions a parade of demure girls, English majors from St. Xavier's or King's College with satin skin and long hair, appropriately endowed with dowries—cash, clothes, jewelry, even property. He's the perfect suitor for some unsuspecting, marriage-hungry girl, Surya muses, who must save her family from the disgrace of maidenhood.

Surya's life had been different. She'd fallen in love the very night she saw Vijay at the club, New Year's Eve, seven years ago. She'd gone up to the bandstand to request "Autumn Leaves," that sweet plaintive tune that always made her heart ache. She hoped her last-minute date and the office gang at Table 75 would approve of her choice. Vijay was in the queue too, ahead of her; wearing a smart sports jacket over dark slacks, and as he stepped forward, she heard him say, "Nat King Cole's Autumn Leaves."

"Okay, one Nat King Cole coming up," the bandleader said, "right after two Humperdincks and three Dean Martins."

"I can wait," Vijay grinned, stepping aside. "It's my favorite song."

The bandleader looked enquiringly at Surya. "I-uh-was about to request the same song," Surya said, suddenly embarrassed. Vijay smiled. "It's my favorite too," she added, almost defensively.

That was fate, she'd decide seven years later, not coincidence. Surya believed coincidences yielded confusion, something she evaded in her orderly world. She believed in fate. Only fate brought people together, only fate pulled them apart.

Tonight she puts fresh flowers on the table and stands in the balcony waiting for the blue sedan to turn at the culvert. She'd talked their daughter into spending the night with her grandmother across town.

"She'll let you roll nice whole-wheat *puris,*" she'd said enticingly, as she packed Anita's Mickey Mouse pajamas, matching toothbrush, barrettes and snuggly slippers. Vijay had bought them on his last trip to the States.

Tonight she fixes something Vijay loves—tandoori chicken, *parattas* stuffed with lentils, chocolate mousse for dessert. He'd mentioned it was a light workday. The biannual plant inspection was almost done, logs updated, the sales quota exceeded. Things would ease up, she hoped; perhaps they could watch a movie together, sleep in late on Saturday. Anita's piano lesson wasn't until noon. Tonight, perhaps, he'd touch her as once he had.

She awakes to sunlight slanting through the window curtains. Two filtered rays fall on the pillow, which still bears the indent of his face. The bathroom light is off. She listens for kitchen sounds—a whistling kettle, the thud of the refrigerator door, a tinkling teaspoon, the flutter of the morning newspaper. Nothing. All is still. She tiptoes to the window, peeks at the garage. Her car has been backed out of the driveway and parked near the coconut tree. It's Saturday; where had he gone? Pulling her *kaftan* over her shoulders she walks barefoot to the kitchen. On a discarded envelope, weighted by a coffee mug is a hurried scrawl: "Sorry about last night. I was exhausted. Forgot about today's executive retreat. I'll be late. V.J."

Surya picked up the mug, twirled it in her hands. On one side was a star-shaped decal with "World's Best Dad" printed in fluorescent blue; on the opposite side a pink heart inscribed with "And Husband." When the mug was filled with a hot liquid, the decals glowed. Surya had bought it the year Anita turned two; now after numerous cups of tea, coffee or hot chocolate the decals had lost their sensitivity to heat. They had stopped glowing.

This morning is the same as any other. Surya fixes Anita's lunch just the way she likes it—American style—peanut butter spread thick on a warm bun, jalapeno cheese crackers, banana and Kit Kat, tucked nicely in her Mickey Mouse lunch box. So much like her father, Surya thinks, kissing her daughter good-bye. She likes her food dry, unmixed and properly identified—no messy curries and soggy lentils sloshing about. The only variables are Almond Joys or Kit Kats, and a choice of Smooth or Extra Crunchy Jiffy peanut butter. Vijay always picked up a couple of jars for his daughter each time he went to New York, which was becoming more and more frequent in the last two years ever since their U.S. collaboration began.

Again today, she drives down Gandhi road, parks in the same spot by the sugarcane juice stand and enters the park to begin her work out. This morning marks the seventh day since *he's* been here, she notes, smoothing her black shorts against her thighs. She double knots her shoes and drapes her Oakley sunglasses on her head like a headband. These she'll wear during the cool down period, the last two laps, to slow her heart and mute the sun against the black shaggy rocks of a teal Arabian Sea.

That night Vijay came home late again, but at least he remembered to phone, or rather, the driver did.

"*Sahib* said meeting is delayed, Madam," he yelled, over the din of traffic.

"Did he say exactly how late?" Instantly, she regretted her razor-edge voice.

"No, Madam," the driver replied, respectfully.

Well, she thought, piling her plate high, he'll just have to eat reheated *pullao*, and it serves him right if the rice grains stick together. The fragrance of cloves, cinnamon, a caramelized topping of fried onions, raisins and slivered almonds made her hungry. She might as well enjoy her food. Who knew when he'd get home? The drive itself was seventy-five minutes on a good day, that's when those mangy cows didn't sit in the middle of the street chewing their cud, or wrinkled pedestrians weren't bungling across every few yards. Of course, Vijay would have had his first drink in the car itself. He kept ice in a thermos flask, a pint of Jack Daniel's under the seat.

"Why not?" he'd shot back, when she'd questioned his wisdom. *He* wasn't driving; it wasn't against the law, and it eased the pain in his back on the long ride home.

"But on an empty stomach?" she'd pressed.

"It's not empty," he'd snapped. "There's always a bag of snacks—salted peanuts, spicy couscous, potato chips, whatever. The driver knows his job."

Surya had backed down. That was just one more worry she could do nothing about—his recent drinking. Too many worries, she thought, gathering like cobwebs in the corners of her mind.

She wiped her mouth and sipped her lemon water, wishing she could sweep them all away. The rice really was delicious—too bad that by the time he'd kick off his shoes, pour another drink and click on CNN, it would turn to a cold paste.

Again, for the ninth consecutive morning *he* isn't here, she thinks rounding the corner on her third lap. She wonders if he's returned to the States, or perhaps he's in another town at his wedding. Perhaps he'd held his bride's hand, intricately patterned in fiery red henna and circled the fire seven times as priests chanted and incense rose—she in a red and gold *sari*, braid entwined with jasmine—he like a dark horse in a white and gold silk *kurta*, open at the neck. Perhaps their wedding bed had been sprinkled with red rose petals. Perhaps her skin was soft, her breasts and belly firm to his touch. Surya glanced surreptitiously over her shoulder toward the entrance gate and caught herself. She shook her head vigorously as if to shake her thoughts free. What was the matter with her? There was much on her mind, way too much, to warrant such adolescent fantasy. She must get home quickly, rush to the bazaar, and prepare the evening meal for Vijay and his colleagues.

"Make it a little less spicy," he'd called, rushing out the door. "Two guys are New Yorkers."

Earlier, he'd asked her to cook *biryani*—both vegetarian with peas and non-vegetarian with tender mutton chunks. And of course, the usual dessert—Kwality pistachio ice cream. It was the creamiest by far.

"And how about chocolate mousse too?" he'd added, as an afterthought. "It tasted great last week."

Surya nodded, sure. That was hardly a problem, but she wished he'd said a word of appreciation then. Vijay also wanted the house spotless, he'd said, fresh flowers in the foyer, their good china, plenty of ice for cocktails. Could her mother keep Anita for the evening again? Surya reminded herself to turn on the air conditioner so that the house would cool before twilight.

She quickens her pace on the last lap, remembering the day's chores. Already the sun is high, promising a scorching day. Rounding the bend, she veers closer to the stone wall so that she can breathe the salty sea air, feel the spray of big waves thrashing against the rocks below. At the far end beyond the park, the *dhobis* were already at work, thumping yards of colorful *saris* against flat rocks, hanging them out to dry on poles like tents.

Surya slows, then stops abruptly with a cry. Damn, she mutters under her breath, crouching with a sudden, stabbing pain. Grasping her calf, she hobbles to the wall and leans against it, eyes closed, her face to the sea, working the kinks out of her muscle with her fingers.

She doesn't see him until he is beside her—that sudden shock of tar-black hair, the white stripe on blue shorts.

"Hurt?" he asks, and her heart leaps from her chest.

"What?" she asks, taken aback, instantly feeling foolish.

"Are you hurt? Your leg…," he points, "I saw you stumble…"

"Oh, it's just a cramp," she says quickly. "It'll pass."

"Care to sit down?" He points to a park bench in the shade nearby and takes her elbow. Her heart is back in her chest, thumping.

"Maybe, for a minute," Surya says.

"You run everyday?" he asks, after he has wiped the bench with his handkerchief.

"Almost everyday," she nods, smiling, "but you don't."

"No, but I should. I used to in Central Park," he grins. "New York," he explains, seeing her uncertain expression.

Right, Surya thinks. Just as she had guessed, of course. "And you're here—visiting—to get married," she says, surprising herself. And it isn't even a question.

He hesitates. "Actually, I ..."

"I'm sorry," she says, recovering quickly. "That was rude. We haven't even introduced ourselves. I'm Surya."

"Pradeep," he says, shaking her hand, oddly. He smiles. "No, actually I'm not. Not married, that is." He grins. "Just here on business."

'Yeah, the business of interviewing eligible hopefuls,' Surya thinks to herself. She nods, looking away. "For long?" she asks, trying to sound casual, afraid he might read her mind.

"Another month at least," he says. "Then back and forth till the business settles. It's tough in the beginning."

"And speaking of business," she says, rising abruptly, "I—I must be going."

"Perhaps we'll meet again," he says, helping her up. He points to her shoes and grins. "I see you made a double knot."

She is oddly flattered that he would notice, or remember. She smiles, turning in the direction of the exit. When she looks back, he is still standing at the park bench looking at her, framed by a red hibiscus bush.

Everything is in order for Vijay and his guests. On the stove, the *biryani* made with good basmati fills the house with fragrance. The dining table is set for six, a bowl of red roses in the center, and in the background a new CD of Ravi Shankar and Philip Glass. She is wearing a midnight blue silk *sari*.

Surya rises to open the door when she hears the easy chatter of voices on the stairs. Through the peephole, she can see Vijay's face, relaxed, nodding, smiling. It should be a pleasant event, she thinks. Flinging open the door, she catches her breath, her heart in her throat. It doesn't seem possible. The odds are too great. But there is no mistaking it. Behind her husband, her eyes meet and settle on one man—and his head of jet-black hair.

She steps back to welcome them. She has always believed in fate. Only fate brings people together, only fate pulls them apart.

TWO HANDS
TO CLAP

This time, Leela thought, there'll be no surprises. Come Sunday evening, she'd park her Toyota in their two-car garage next to Jeff's 10x8 empty space. His shiny, black Lincoln Mark-8 with its chrome wheels and gleaming emblem would be gone. She'd watch the garage door levitate, nestle under the rafters, then pull in and turn off the engine. At one time, the sight of Jeff's car made her heart literally leap with an oh-good-he's-home kind of joy, and she would run up the driveway, key in hand. But in time, she began to vacillate between indifference and apprehension, not knowing what to expect of herself or him. Ambivalence frightened her. Like a hollow reed, she felt anyone could blow right through her.

She glanced at her watch. It was still early. She could hear the ocean thrashing somewhere in the distance. At a steady hum, it would take her a couple of hours to reach the Chesapeake Bay Bridge, then another 45 minutes on 97N. Vaguely, she wondered if Jeff had left the lawnmower or David's bike in her car space rather than against the wall near the stacked bags of peat moss and holly tone.

Standing in the balcony in her batik nightie, she squinted at the sun's first rays tinting the fog. She slurped a mouthful of strong coffee and held the warm mug to her breast. Sometime during the night, the fog had climbed over the iron railing and crouched into the balcony like a thief. She wished the sun would chase it out before she started for home. Something began to gnaw at the fringes of her mind. Suppose Jeff hadn't left by the time she got home? What if he was still packing?

"I'll call before I leave," she murmured to herself. If he answered the phone, she'd hang up although that wasn't her style. And what if he guessed it was she? Well, at least she'd avoid a potentially awkward situation.

Leela finished her coffee and changed into jeans and a sweat-shirt. She would go for one last walk on the beach. She pressed "L" on the elevator panel and walked along the promenade, past Sandy House, past the outdoor kiddy pool, now dry like a crater, a "Closed" sign swinging in the crisp autumn air. Fifteen years ago, they had rented a first floor apartment here so David could scamper down to the beach. Pulling on the hood of her sweat shirt, she tied a knot under her chin and walked briskly down the wooden planks, then on to pristine white sand. Damp air clung to her throat, thick and clammy, like the rice poultice her mother put on her chest when she got bronchitis.

She recalled another morning on Falcon Island. Leaving David at Kiddy Camp, she and Jeff escaped for a walk by them-selves. The tide was coming in, lashing against the embankment with relentless persistence. The sound of the sea, rough and cal-lous, still rumbled in her ears.

"Let's build a fortress," Jeff had said, impulsively. "Let's stop the tide."

Her response was instinctive. "Okay. Right here?"

And they had spent the next few hours constructing an elaborate embankment fortified with broken shell and barnacle-encrusted black stones. Valiantly, it had withstood the onslaught, at least for several magical minutes, and between each gush of foam and froth, they worked frantically rebuilding eroded walls. In the end, of course, the whole thing toppled, leaving them exhausted, dripping with globs of sand, strangely elated. Walking back silently, arms linked, they promised to return. Dreams came easy then. Two years later, even before David could punch "4" on the elevator, they'd made a small down payment on a two bedroom unit.

Leela bent to pick up a sand dollar. What she'd most loved about Jeff was the way he flung crazy ideas about, like confetti. She had always been level headed, a linear, focused thinker ploughing rough career terrain, successful by anyone's standards. But it was Jeff who made her laugh with his spontaneous big-joke-attitude to life. And so, when he proposed marriage with the same let's-go-for-it- kind of abandon with which he'd barred the tide, she stalled, wary of a rush of freedom. They had been walking beneath a thick overhang of red oaks in Willow Creek Park toward a clear stream where earlier, Jeff had immersed a six-pack of Coke. Their picnic basket packed with sandwiches—rare roast beef for him, cheese and chutney for her, and a fresh fruit salad to share, was propped against a weeping willow.

"But how can we get married?" she'd asked, miserable with reality.

"Why not? The whole world does," he'd grinned.

"It's too complex," she'd said. "Exchange visitor visas can't be renewed, and. . ."

But he wasn't listening. "So? Wait for me. Just four years, then I'll go with you."

"To New Delhi?" she asked, voice incredulous. "You'll never survive. And, how will we. . ." She stopped, overwhelmed by the enormity of it all.

"In an airplane," he answered. Laughing, he swooped the palms of his hand upward like the nose of a Boeing 747, and landed them on her shoulders. He kissed her tenderly. "Say yes," he whispered. "Please say yes."

Just then a red cardinal overhead relieved himself, barely missing Jeff's shoulder. White slime splattered on top of his shoe. Leela dissolved into a splutter of giggles as he bent to wipe it off with dry leaves.

"Okay, that's done then," Jeff grinned. He pointed to the white smear on his shoe. "We've even been blessed. See?"

"But what about our parents, what will they. . .?"

He grinned again. "I don't know," he said. "But here's what I do know." Clasping his hands in a pathetic imitation of Pavarotti, he belted out a song with exaggerated emotion.

"Birdie, oh birdie... in the sky...

Dropped a whitie in my eye

Me don't worry, me don't cry

Me just glad that cows can't fly."

Leela wiped her eyes. Twenty-three years gone since he'd concocted that poem, his shoe the color of aluminum, his eyes like polished onyx. It wasn't anyone's fault. Shit happens. How often had she read those bumper stickers? It would've been easier if she could pinpoint reasons, logical explanation, something coherent to explain to her family. She practiced different expressions.

"Doesn't care."

"He's never here."

"Drinks too much ..."

"He's seeing someone else. . ."

Great opening sentences, a prelude to counseling, therapy, or whatever married people resort to when marriages falter. But none applied to her. And there wasn't enough of anything left over—relief, grief, or regrets, to fill a thimble. Nothing at all. What did her mother always say? It takes two hands to clap. You couldn't fight someone who didn't fight back, and if you didn't fight about anything, there'd be peace. At least a semblance of it. The axiom had worked for her parents; ironically they'd even been happy, as happiness goes. Her father believed he knew everything, and said little to prove or disprove it. Even his anger was controlled, one-liners delivered with the piercing accuracy of a bowman, right through a deer's heart. Her mother rarely replied, at least not audibly. Under the guise of serenity, she believed in withholding all argument especially in front of her children. Marriage and family life were valuables to be preserved like antiques at any cost, including one's happiness. As far as Leela could tell, her mother hadn't been particularly unhappy or happy for the thirty-eight years of her marriage, and now as a widow, she lived on the same even keel. Why, Leela wondered, could she not achieve her mother's tranquility?

"Men," her mother once explained, "*need* to feel like kings."

"Why?" Leela wanted to know.

"Because they do. It's in their nature. And it's our job to treat them that way," she added softly.

"But it's demeaning," Leela cried. "Don't we have a right to be happy? Why must it be tied to men?"

Her mother looked up, eyes profoundly sad. "It doesn't have to be," she said. "But it is. Because they make sure it is."

Leela said nothing more. Jeff was different, unassuming. They had raised David together, precariously balancing careers and parental obligations, sharing the triumphs and perils of his adolescent years. And yet, the spark between them had fizzled and died. Not that that was uncommon in marriages, but to Leela's bewilderment, Jeff was nonchalant, even fatalistic and philosophical about it, content to play golf or watch it on TV, and *that's* what she couldn't accept, what hurt the most. She would not buy that love, like the natural progression of life, could only die. And so she pursued their relationship as if it were a course of study. They'd taken lessons in ballroom dancing, French cooking, automechanics, computers. She'd permed her hair and lost fifteen pounds. She planned a cruise to the Virgin Islands. But, in her heart she knew she was clapping with one hand.

Leela stopped. A sea gull stood blithely beside a soup tureen, an inverted horseshoe crab, drinking deeply. In some ways, Leela felt like that arthropod, upside down and drained of her innards. She thought about David. He was in college now. How would he react? Of course, it would hurt, but then David was pragmatic. She recalled the time she turned down a fellowship in New York because her second pregnancy was at risk. When she lost the baby, David had comforted her about both losses. He watched her aspirations, as some boys watch baseball, keeping score, aware that her dual identity was equally defined by work and motherhood. And *that's* why he'd find the separation ludicrous. Were she to leave on promotion or some assignment, he'd understand the logic, Leela thought. But a no-reason reason would make no sense.

Leela looked at her watch and stopped abruptly. She had walked over two miles, without realizing it. The fog had burned. The Falcon water tower loomed before her, silently beckoning. The beach was bare. She shuddered, stuck her hands in her pockets and turned, half running back.

The phone was ringing as she unlocked the door. She grabbed the receiver, her heart racing ahead of her feet. It went dead. She turned to pick up her bags, just as the sharp ring began again.

David's voice was cheerful. "Hey Mom. What's up? What you doing at the beach by yourself?"

"Where are you?" Leela's heart contracted. She had been sure it was Jeff, especially after the phone went dead.

"Home," he said. "I called last night and got Dad. He said he wouldn't be here today. Something about a meeting in Philadelphia."

"How come you're home?" she asked, foolishly.

"Just felt like driving home for the weekend," he said. "I finished exams. Thought I'd spend some old quality time with my favorite mother." He sounded happy, relaxed. "And while I'm at it, I'll get in a round of golf with Dad."

"I'm sorry," she murmured. "Maybe Uncle Kevin can play with you."

"Oh no, that's okay," David said, "Dad'll be back Sunday. I won't leave till after dinner."

Leela gulped. "I don't think so," she whispered hoarsely. "Dad and I. . ."

"I know, I know," David interrupted. "Dad told me. You guys were to drive up to New York and see Grandma after the Philly meeting, but since you went to the beach, he'll just come on home."

Leela's heart was in her mouth. "He said *that?*"

"Said what? What's wrong with you, Mom? You're weirder than usual." His voice rippled, "When are you coming home, anyway?"

Leela swallowed hard. "Now," she answered. "I was about to leave."

"Oh good," David said. "And listen, I had to park in your

spot. It's easier to get the rear end of my jeep in. The lawn mower's on the other side. I'll go move it so you can pull into Dad' spot. See ya soon?"

"Yes, yes," she whispered, laying the receiver down softly in its cradle.

THE BARREN
WINDOW LEDGE

She stood nervously by the window and looked out into the crowded alley below. "I could've sworn I dusted this ledge," she murmured, wiping a cobweb away from her elbow. She flicked at a spider painstakingly weaving a new web between the down spout and the window grating, then turned from habit to reach for a duster and stopped abruptly. No. Not now. She didn't want to take her eyes off the street below. She might miss their arrival.

Twisting her body around the parapet, she cupped her palms like a sun visor over her eyes, leaning over as far as she could. Not much activity at the head of the alley. A stray dog was urinating against the gatepost and the usual masses of people were streaming toward the railway station to catch the 8:00 a.m. local to Victoria Terminal. She dragged her eyes over the spires of Christ Church, and the unlit neon letters "Pfizer Ltd., Bombay," that grazed the top of the Khyber building tower. All the buildings were the same dingy gray except for the gleaming white Church steeple and the flowers on the adjoining terrace. All around the iron grate, variegated coleus in earthenware pots sat like sentries in multicolored uniforms. In the center, an old rusty cauldron overflowed with hibiscus blooms. Two floors below, the new tenants had set out an urn of wandering jew and a large ficus. She had seen them unload it from the Goods Carrier lorry like it was a prize possession. Julie stuck her finger in the planter of baby's tears she had set on her own window ledge. She liked herbs, coriander especially, and fennel. But yesterday at the greenhouse, those tiny, round leaves dripping over slender stems, so like real baby's tears, had made her ache and, impulsively she had bought the plant.

"It's appropriate," she thought, feeling her apprehension lift if only for an instant.

The alley was a dead end street, always crowded, but not as bad as it would get later that evening. Later, people returning from work would dodge past children playing jump rope and hopscotch on the hot tar where thick, yellow chalk lines demarcated their zone of play. Now that a resolution banning rickshaws and taxis from entering the narrow gullies was passed, the children turned the alley into a playground. They even put up badminton nets between two pillars and tossed a shuttlecock around. Julie would often sit by her window and watch the children, invariably rooting for the losing team; whichever one it happened to be. She couldn't help that. She glanced absently at her watch. The morning vendors were beginning to trickle in. Below her, the vegetable woman had rounded the corner and entered the alley. From the heavy basket precariously balanced on her head filled with too many purple *brinjals*, okra and fresh coriander, she assumed the morning had not been particularly profitable. Julie considered calling her upstairs. Keeping a few baby carrots on hand might not be such a bad idea, but then she'd have to abandon her vigil at the window while the woman slowly squatted, brought out her rusty iron scales and enticed her into buying vegetables she didn't want. Julie abandoned her transient, sympathetic illusions. She really did not want to leave the window. Not now. Not after all this time.

Was everything ready? Did she forget something? She surveyed the baby's room in her mind like a fastidious home inspector. She had painted the walls a bright yellow because Mama said yellow felt sunny even in the middle of monsoons. In one corner of the room, stood a new teak bed that Stan, her husband, had insisted on buying, the one with railings. Julie liked simple lines, open spaces. Railings, even if they kept bolsters from toppling over, felt like a prison. But eventually she agreed because the matching chest of drawers with its ornate brass knobs and the small, unique carved rocker won her heart. She had put five sets of underwear, three pairs of shorts with matching interchangeable tops, a flowered pinafore, a sailor girl outfit and lots of pairs of socks, in the first two drawers and, in the third drawer, wrapped in fine muslin, a white sweater she had tenderly knitted herself. She hadn't known how to knit but she bought a simple pattern, mostly pearls and plains, and patiently taught herself. Now, all she had to do was attach the sleeves to the main body of the garment. It had turned out prettier than she had envisioned. Julie loved white even if it wasn't practical. In another corner by the east window, overlooking the bougainvillea trellis, sat the almost life sized doll that came with a feeding bottle and the ability to cry when her stomach was pressed. That, she hoped, would really break the ice. After all, what little girl could resist comforting a baby doll?

The thought of the feeding bottle jolted her from her reverie.

Turning abruptly from the window, she called, "Stan. Stan, did you get the milk?"

"What milk?"

"Milk. You know, milk for the baby. For porridge and. . ."

"You didn't say anything about milk. I bought the gripe water you asked for. And the Quaker Oats."

"But all babies drink milk, Stan. I didn't think I had to spell *that* out."

He walked in and stood in the doorway, his deep-set eyes pensive under thick, bushy eyebrows. He wore a pair of comfortable tan slacks and his favorite cream shirt with the embroidered palm tree on the pocket.

Julie looked up. "You know, you could've worn what you had on yesterday," she began, her voice sharp. "After all, I won't have time to wash and iron like I've been doing. I'll have to bathe and feed her and. . . " She stopped, suddenly. "What if she doesn't sleep, Stan?" she asked, her voice quivering. "What if she cries all night? For Maggie and the other children. She's not used to being an only child."

Stanley walked across the living room and put his arms around her shoulders. She was cold despite the sunshine pouring in through the window. He took her hands and rubbed them in his.

"Maggie says Annie sleeps on her tummy. That's okay isn't it?" she asked. "I mean, she's too old to suffocate." Glancing up, she caught Stan wincing. "Babies do, Stan. You have to be careful with blankets and pillows. Maggie says she sucks her thumb so hard, there's a callus on her knuckle. I read somewhere that's a sign of insecurity. But I think Annie's just hungry. Don't you?" Stanley smiled at his wife and nodded. "And you know what?" Julie continued, "Maggie says Annie doesn't wet her bed. Only sometimes, after a bad dream." Her voice rose. "I didn't think babies had bad dreams. Do you? I mean, what bad thing. . ."

Stanley touched her cheek. "I wish you'd stop worrying," he began, but she had turned back to the window murmuring, "I wonder what's keeping them. They'd said sometime around eight. The bus from Poona comes into the depot by seven, then it's another hour by taxi. You know, Stan, we should've gone. Didn't I say we should meet them at the depot? But no, Maggie insisted it wasn't good for Annie." She turned her face to him, defiantly. "Why wouldn't it be good? I mean, how would the baby know?"

"Julie, it's only a little past eight. Maybe…"

"Maybe there was an accident," she interrupted. "Maybe they haven't even left Poona yet. I mean, how would we know? No one in our building has a phone."

"Only businesses are eligible for phone connections," Stanley said, patiently. "You know that."

"Even if Maggie sent a telegram, it won't reach till tomorrow," Julie said. She walked swiftly into the baby's room. Pulling open the third drawer of the teak dresser, she untied the muslin knot and lifted the white sweater. Carefully, she carried it to her high-backed chair by the window and spread it out on her lap. She could feel her spirits plummeting in a free fall, and the only way to stop it, she knew, was to concentrate deeply on something— almost anything. Sometimes, in the past, she'd chop an onion, some garlic and ginger, and begin cooking for no one in particular. Other times she'd settle a closet or a drawer even it didn't need settling.

"May as well start on these sleeves," she murmured. Anything to keep the bottom from falling, she thought to herself. She noted that Stanley had settled in his armchair with the *Times of India*. From the corner of her eye she watched him fold it in quarters to a handy size and crease it down. Little furrows gathered on his forehead as his eyes focused on the black and white checks of the daily crossword.

"Ah, these clues," he said. "They're merciless, today. I've never been so shut out. Even the anagrams are difficult." He let out a long drawn out sigh.

She watched him reread a clue and close his eyes. What was he thinking? She knew he'd never wanted a child as much as she had. Not that it mattered, because she didn't conceive anyway, despite repeated attempts. Even now, she sometimes wondered whose fault it had been.

"You think we should have adopted a baby?" she blurted out, suddenly.

Stanley's eyes burst open. "What?"

"A baby," Julie said. "I'm wondering if we should have…"

Stanley put the paper down on the floor. "Now, what's bringing this on?"

Julie sucked her breath in. "Just answer the question, Stan."

"Maybe," he said. "But adoptions are risky, too."

"Exactly. It's like Lucky Dip."

She was referring to their childhood memories of the City Fair, where kids, for a small price, could dip into a barrel of wrapped toys and pull one out. You had to keep your eyes closed, and you couldn't feel around the packages.

Stan smiled. "Well, it's not *that* bad. But it would have been cleaner than what we're getting ourselves into now."

Julie stopped clicking her needles. "What do you mean? These types of arrangements are common among families. I thought you *liked* Maggie," she bristled. "At least, better than Rosie. You always say my older sister is moodier than me."

"Yes, but Rosie's trustworthy. Not manipulative like.." The words shot out of his mouth, across the room, grazing Julie's heart.

Julie burst into tears. "Stan, why are you..? Is this the time to bring this up? Speaking ill of Maggie when we're waiting for her? And Annie, too?"

Stan rose quickly and came to her. "I'm sorry," he said, handing her his handkerchief. "I didn't mean it like that." He put his arm around her shoulders. "The thing is, you are so sweet and trusting. You never see anything wrong with anyone, least of all, your family." He kissed the top of her head and returned to his crossword.

Julie wiped her eyes, rose from her chair and went back to guarding the window, squinting in the sunlight. Not that Maggie was difficult to spot. She was a big boned woman with broad, capable shoulders, ample breasts and large pelvic bones designed to produce babies. And this she did—three boys, two girls and another due in six months. Julie didn't know what to think of such indiscretion. She recalled her sister's face—strong jaw, and a generous, almost voluptuous mouth that yielded a surprisingly sparse harvest of tight smiles. But then, who could smile with so many babies? She remembered how sick Maggie had become during her last pregnancy. For the final six weeks, she had stayed in Bombay occupying the room now painted yellow. And after Annie's birth, things deteriorated further. First, Annie developed jaundice. Julie would bundle up the child under her raincoat and carry her to a waiting taxi each morning, back to the hospital, for her UV treatment. Shortly thereafter, Annie contracted pneumonia. Each night she burned with a violent fever and her chest was so congested Julie could hear her labored breathing over the constant pouring rain. That was when the monsoons pounded the coastline and there was nothing anyone could do to relieve the dank mustiness that settled in the house and crept through the crevices at night like the cockroaches. Julie saw them scurrying along the kitchen counter when she woke to give Annie her 2 a.m. medicine. Carefully, she'd pour the chalky pink liquid in a teaspoon and feed it drop by drop, watching the tiny mouth suck long after the last drop was gone. She'd change her diaper and lay her in a crib they had borrowed from the woman upstairs. And then she'd watch over her, humming a few strains of Brahms lullaby until she fell asleep. Sometimes, if she didn't, Julie would bring her over to her own bed rather than wake Maggie up. She was certain Maggie wouldn't mind especially since she put her back in the crib before her 6 o'clock feed. And if the child nestled against her breast and sucked her nipples a little, how was that any different from a pacifier? And where was it necessary to tell Maggie or anyone for that matter? Julie felt her body stir under her clothes. It had been almost two years since Maggie had returned to Poona with the child. Nothing had changed. Annie still suffered from chronic asthma attacks, and despite herbal compresses, homeopathic medicine and Lourdes miracle water, the problem had escalated.

And then, Maggie had written, "Maybe she'll do better in Bombay. Would you take her for a while? The doctor thinks the change will do her good, but with this new baby coming..."

Julie's heart had soared right out of her rib cage. But Stanley's eyes had been grave and solemn. Like an owl peering into the dark alley.

"I'm not sure this is a good idea for us," he'd said, "Especially for you."

"Why not?" Julie had blurted, much too anxiously. "What's so awful about that? Annie knows us, sort of, she might even remember me—I mean, you too, and—and it would help Maggie." She gulped. "It's only for a few months." She looked down at the gold band she was wearing, and paused. "For a few months Stan, or—or maybe a little longer?"

She'd tried to hide the longing, the near panic that had risen like smoke from that cold spot in her chest up through her trembling voice. And yet she knew, she had unveiled her barrenness. In the way her brown eyes had turned to brick at Stan's gentle resistance. In the halting way she had gestured with her small expressive hands like a pantomime. And later, that night, in the smooth firmness of her belly untarnished by stretch marks, glistening under his gaze.

The next day, she sent Maggie a telegram and bustled about, emptying the yellow room, singing softly to herself. She tried not to think about the woman in their village who'd actually donated her baby to her sister to sort of keep, indefinitely. Maggie would never do that, of course. She wasn't that kind of sister. Or was she? Maybe, if she was tired enough, maybe if Annie's health really improved, it just might work out that way. But, no, that's certainly not what Julie wanted for herself. She was sure, "cross-my-heart-and-hope-to-die" sure, she thought brooding, recalling how she and Maggie had once signed childhood pledges.

Now, she peered through the sunlight. Old Mrs. D'cruz was limping back from church, her black rosary still entwined around her gnarled knuckles. Julie leaped across the room in four strides.

"Oh, I just remembered something Stan." She spoke rapidly. "You know Brian D'cruz who lives across from Christ Church? He was due to arrive today."

"From where?"

"From Poona, of course. I met his mother in the bazaar yesterday. She said Brian was in Poona finalizing the sale of their property. He was to return today." She tugged on his arm. "Stan, listen. Go down there and ask. See if he's home. Maybe he saw Maggie hail a cab." Stan looked doubtfully at her. "Well, at least then we'll know if the bus was on time," Julie said defensively, "and—and maybe, the traffic on the bridge is —" Her voice rose. "That's it. That must be it. Oh, they should have come via the tunnel. You know how Saturdays are!" Stan remained quiet. "Saturday mornings, the flower bazaar near Nehru bridge is—is worse than the cemetery on All Soul's Day," Julie asserted. "Baskets of rose petals, marigold and jasmine garlands everywhere. People stop right in the middle to buy flowers for *puja*." She coaxed. "Go on. Stan, please go." *The Times* slid to the floor. "And hurry," she called, as Stan hesitated. Slowly, he unbolted the front door leading to the verandah and stepped out into the hallway. Julie latched the door, returned to the window and plopped down in her chair.

The noon Angelus began to chime. Slowly, Julie lifted her head from the cushion and instinctively made the sign of the cross, then stopped. What had happened? She must have dozed off in the warm morning sun. She stretched and suddenly remembered. Where was Maggie? And the baby? Why hadn't they arrived yet? And Stan, where on earth was Stan? He'd been gone nearly two hours! She jumped up and leaned over the parapet. She rubbed her eyes with her fingertips, adjusted them to the morning glare. There! There he was! He had just turned the corner and entered the alley, walking slowly in measured footsteps like an old man, his head bowed, shoulders hunched forward, hands hanging at his sides. Like a scarecrow. Empty.

Julie felt her heart constrict as she watched her husband. Instinctively, she knew. Maggie had changed her mind. The multi-colored coleus on the terrace opposite spilled over the urns into pools of water. She bent over the ledge, picked up her planter of baby's tears and the beautiful white sweater from the chair. She walked quietly into the baby's yellow room. Sitting cross-legged on the floor near the rocker, she lay the sweater down carefully in her lap and beginning at the bottom, began to undo each stitch.

Pearl, plain, pearl, plain.

Row by row by row.

Leaf by leaf by leaf.

THE ARRANGEMENT

Two days have passed since Suresh's arrival in India, and already, America seems even further away than it is. He turns over in bed and pulls the sheet up to his chin. You can't go any further than halfway around the world, he thinks, and yet, coming home is like stepping off the edge of the earth. He closes his eyes, listening to the sing-song of peddlers selling vegetables—*brinjal*, okra, gourds—which sound unfamiliar, and fruit like guavas and pomegranates, he hasn't eaten in a long while. He knows his mother will call the vendors upstairs to the door to buy the day's supply of fresh produce. The raspy voice of the fisherwoman touting the morning's catch floats through the window. Already, he can smell *ghee* sizzling over puffed up, fragrant balloons of dough. *Puris* and potato *bhaji*, his favorite breakfast, is well underway. He listens as his mother admonishes the cook not to make the food too spicy.

"My son is home from America," she says, "his stomach is not made of iron, like yours. Remember, I told you to put less chilies and more coconut in the *masala*."

"*Aiy*, I'm so sorry I forgot," the old woman replies, flustered.

"Forgot? How can *anyone* forget Suresh baba is home? Here, let me do that. You take these clothes to the *dhobhi* and tell him to be careful. Be gentle, don't pound them too much. The material is light. Tell him, they're from America," she says, as if the washerwoman, like the cook, should have heard of America. "And we need them back in two days. My son can't stay long— he's just picking a girl and going back."

"*Aiy*, that's too sad," the old woman says, "When will the marriage be?"

"*Arey*, let him find a girl first. How much will you talk? Go on, take this bundle of clothes and hurry back. And buy a dozen red roses from that *phool walla* at the corner. Make sure the petals aren't turning black," she adds, counting out several dog-eared rupee notes.

Suresh listens as the woman shuffles along, her *chappals* flapping down the cement steps and out into the garden below his window. He yawns, stretching his long legs, wishing he could have slept naked as he did in America. But his room here isn't as private, and of course, Amy isn't here either. He closes his eyes again, letting his imagination go unfettered, wild and wonderful. Their last night together, she'd thrown her legs around him and sat astride, bending forward, watching him arch his body, looking at the madness of the full moon in his eyes. No matter how passionate their love-making, he knew she'd never understand why he had to leave.

She was in the kitchen the next morning fixing breakfast—a Mexican style omelet with cheese and chunky salsa.

"It's just a formality Amy," he'd said, trying again to explain his predicament. "Foreign educated Indian men, especially doctors, are like trophies that girls back home want to win. At least, their well-connected families do. My mother says marriage proposals have been pouring in. She wants me to come home and, at least, pretend to be interested," he'd said, kissing the nape of her neck. "You know, just play the game—go through the process, so important people don't take offense."

"Ah, so you're a sizzling hot commodity?" Amy had half-teased.

"You might say that. And *you* ought to know," he'd added, his lips on her earlobes.

"Not now, Suresh. I have to get ready for work." Amy had said, flipping the omelet on a plate. "And, this will get cold." She put two slices of multigrain bread in the toaster.

His fingers moved up the front of her nightie. "So? Let it get cold."

"Stop it," she'd said, smacking his fingers. "Maybe, tonight. What time is your flight tomorrow?"

"Are you kidding? Did you say *maybe*? Sweetheart, I'm afraid you'll have to do without your beauty sleep tonight. And you won't be sorry, I promise." He'd kissed her lightly on the cheek and sat at the breakfast bar. Amy poured herself a cup of coffee and joined him.

"So you guys marry without dating?" Her voice was incredulous.

"Right. Not in the technical sense. The families meet and if the couple-to-be "like" each other—whatever that means—a deal is struck. Nowadays, couples might go out once or twice alone, but not in my parent's generation. And my grandparents *first saw* each other at their marriage ceremony, and then too, Nani's face was covered with her *sari*." He'd burst out laughing. "How's that for progress?"

Amy shook her head. "I don't understand it. How many girls

are you going to interview?"

"I've asked Ma to do the initial screening and pick the best three," Suresh said. "That's all I can handle in one week."

Amy put her coffee cup in the sink. "You'll miss our six-month anniversary," she'd said. "The day we met in the cafeteria line and you bumped my elbow. I'm still waiting for you to replace my cream blouse."

"We'll celebrate as soon as I return. Dinner, movies, new blouse—or no blouse? I like you best in your birthday clothes." He'd walked over to the sink and kissed her hard, feeling her softness against his shirt. "Look, I'm only doing this to appease my mother, Amy. To get her off my back. I'll be back in no time. This is just a dumb formality."

"Eat. Eat more," Suresh's mother says now, placing a puffed-up *puri* on Suresh's plate. "It's going to be a long day."

Suresh watches the oil glisten on the dough as it slowly deflates and the aroma wafts up to his face. He tries to ignore how much he misses home-cooked Indian meals. "Today, you'll meet Gita Gupta," his mother says, "She's the first of the girls you'll see on this trip. Quite beautiful, and she's going to be a doctor, like you. Very modern girl, but traditional too. She'll fit in with your American friends." She emphasizes the word American.

"How do you know what Americans are like, Ma?" Suresh asks. "You haven't met any."

"Yes, I have, at the Bombay Club. Now that Rajiv Gandhi has opened up trade, they're coming in. Friendly people. White, very good looking …and rich.."

"But? There's a—but lurking there."

"Yes, but—well they're not our kind." She hesitates, driving home her point. "Not the kind to marry."

Suresh lets it pass. Not that he'd intended to mention Amy on this trip home. Clearly, it isn't the right time, although he isn't sure when that time will come.

"I know what you're thinking," his mother says, pouring sweet milky *chai* into a strainer. She drops an extra cardamom pod into his mug. "It won't be like last year. I was really careful."

Suresh nods. They'd gone all out that day, on his last trip home, preparing the house as if it was *Divali*—the festival of lights. They'd put up new draperies; the tailor had sewn new cushion covers to match. A stunning new brass urn had appeared in the entry hallway, and there was food enough to feed a small nation. They'd really wanted it to work; they'd expected him to do his part. But he'd turned the girl down. She'd been pretty enough, appropriately docile and feminine, almost too feminine, he thought, recalling her breasts and wide pelvis, tailor-made for popping babies out. She'd been well mannered too and sweet really—yet *something* was missing from the start. Americans called it chemistry, but it wasn't even that. Only much later, after he'd returned to the States, had he pinned it down. In any case, he couldn't possibly have explained it to his parents, so he'd latched on to something tangible.

"I don't know how we missed it," his mother says now, apologetically. "I didn't see her thumb was flat. And her voice was fine when we spoke. No tremors, no stammering, nothing. She must have been nervous with you."

"It doesn't matter, Ma," Suresh says. "It's okay, really. It wasn't meant to be."

What Suresh had told no one—what he'd seen clearly in the twilight that evening as they strolled in the garden before dinner, was his life unfolding in chapters of utter boredom with an obedient, respectful "yes-yes-*ji*" kind-of-woman, and a bunch of brats in tow, all yokes around his neck. A life as dull as ditch water, as predictable as the monsoons in June.

He turns now to his mother, who is watching him with moist eyes. "So, is Gita Gupta your favorite?" he asks, trying to humor her.

"Well, your father and I have no favorites. We just want what's best for you—choose wisely and be happy."

Suresh can't resist. "You mean, *you* want to choose."

His words spread like rain clouds over her face. She looks at him, then out into the open courtyard, where a pair of sparrows is drinking from tea-colored puddles left by the rain. "Is *this* what they teach you in America?" she asks.

Gita is dressed in a plum colored sari with embroidered lavender flowers along the border. Suresh is sure his mother must be disappointed. Most girls came with three-inch-wide gold or silver-bordered *saris* and wore lots of jewelry as a preview of the dowry. Gita wears a single string of amethysts around her neck and delicate earrings. Her black hair hangs down her back in a loose braid with a string of jasmine woven in. From the burnished red highlights around her face, he knows she's put fresh henna into her hair. A closed, polite smile plays on her lips as the late afternoon wears on and the light turns golden over the heavy aroma of garlic and cumin emanating from the kitchen.

The mothers carry the day telling stories that illuminate their children's accomplishments. The fathers sit aside with their whiskey and spicy snacks blowing political steam and tooting their own business horns. Gita sits beside her mother, like a goddess in a temple, watching a circus of earthlings perform. Occasionally, she nods her head and pretends to listen. But every now and then, she looks up and holds his gaze, her eyes like gems, refusing to look away in modest embarrassment, as most Indian girls do.

"I had gone home to my parent's house in Rajasthan for Suresh's birth," his mother is saying, "a small town with just one hospital. Nothing unusual happened there, till Suresh was born— a giant—ten pounds, nine ounces. Such a big, big boy," she holds out her hands to show his size. "People couldn't believe it. All the doctors and nurses, even the X-ray technicians came to see him," she laughs heartily, as if she's telling the story for the first time.

"Well, the big boy has grown into a fine young man," Gita's mother says, smiling at Suresh, who wants to get out of his chair and suture his mother's mouth shut. Instead, he grins and says, "Thank you. It's my mother's favorite story, and I can't even verify it."

"Oh, it's true, *beta*. Really," his mother gushes. Then turning to Mrs. Gupta, she says, "And you have a beautiful *and* smart daughter. Beauty with brains. What is your medical specialty, *beti?*"

Suresh catches Gita's eye and wishes he could make his mother disappear. "I haven't decided yet," Gita says. "Maybe Emergency Medicine, or Gynecology."

"Ma, she doesn't have to decide on a specialty *now*. That comes *after* basic medical school," Suresh bursts out, before he can stop himself. He wonders why Gita hadn't bothered to clarify her indecision.

"Oh, oh, I see. Of course." his mother says, unperturbed. "Suresh is going to be a card—cardio—logist," she adds, her pride spilling over. "Expert in matters of the heart." Her eyes take in Gita and Suresh without any attempt at subtlety.

"I'm thinking about my stomach right now," Suresh says, looking in the direction of the kitchen, where he spies the cook standing behind the curtain, signaling his mother. "I think you are being paged, Ma," he says.

Lunch is served in the spacious dining room. In the center of the table is an arrangement of flowers, fruit and candles surrounded by sand-colored placemats embroidered with sprays of herbs. Matching napkins folded into lotus buds are placed in the center of the plates. A wide array of finger food, tandoori chicken, cucumber salad, yogurt and chutneys are laid out.

Suresh's father pours the wine for everyone and raises his glass. "To family," he says, looking at Gita's parents. "Yours and ours."

Everyone, except Suresh and Gita echo the salutation back. Gita picks at her food, alternating small bites of chicken and cucumber. She eats the spicy potato-filled center of a *samosa* leaving behind deep-fried pieces of crispy dough.

"Gita *beti*," Suresh's mother says, addressing her as daughter for the second time that evening. "Have one more *samosa*, or at least another *pakora*. Come on, don't be shy."

"No, thank you, I'm full," Gita says.

"More chutney? You like this kind—tamarind, the brown one, or coconut—this green chutney?" She pushes both *vatis* closer to Gita. "Which one you tried?"

"The tamarind, thanks. It was delicious."

"Oh, then, you must try the coriander-coconut one," she says, and without waiting, forks a *samosa* and plunks it down on Gita's plate. "Goes good with *samosa*," she smiles, lavishly spooning green chutney over it.

"She doesn't eat much," Gita's mother bursts out. "She eats like a bird, just little here, little there."

"A beautiful bird," Suresh's father adds, appreciatively.

"Oh certainly," Suresh's mother joins in. "But you must eat *beti*; you must eat well. You have to be strong."

Suresh looks at his mother. Strong for what, she didn't say, though everyone knew she meant childbirth. From the corner of his eyes, Suresh glances at Gita. Her eyes are on her plate.

"Young people, especially girls—they don't eat much," his mother continues, turning to Mrs. Gupta. "Not like us. I mean, not like me."

"Not like me too," Mrs. Gupta says. The two women laugh heartily.

"You might say that," Suresh's father chimes in, joining in the laughter. "But still—we're in the company of beautiful ladies, wouldn't you say Mr. Gupta?"

Gita's father guffaws. "Absolutely. How can I deny it?" Mrs. Gupta shoots him a warning smile as if she knows what's coming. "Would I even dare?"

A volley of laughter fills the air. "Oh, well now," Mrs. Gupta says, "you both don't see how lucky you are. The eyes are the first to go with old men," she laughs, turning to Suresh's mother. "Then the brain, or you-know-what."

"Ah, but you are a brave man, Mr. Gupta. Brave, indeed," Suresh's father says, wiping his eyes.

Only later does Suresh recall every detail of these moments with pristine clarity. Only if you were really attuned to a person, would you have detected a red flicker of anger, an instantaneous burst of light, quick as a firefly, there and gone, almost before it ignited. He'd seen it in Gita's eyes when his mother had plunked the *samosa* down on her plate, although she'd politely refused it. Only if you could rise like smoke above the superficial chatter could you hear Gita's heart thumping with anger in her chest, her vein pulsing at her temple, her jaw clenched. He saw the way she jabbed the *samosa* and split it open with her fork, her lips pursed in a thin line. And then, because she knew he'd been watching her, gravely and intently, she'd raised her eyes to his, over the plates and the glasses, the laughter and the know-it-all conversation of their parents, who were discussing her as she were a peach in the fruit bowl at the table. And in her transparent eyes he saw something he didn't expect to see—at least not on a day like today—a blatant contempt for the entire process she had condescended to participate in. And she was daring him to call her on it, to expose her to their parents. Behind the innocent smile lurked a smirk; behind the doe eyes were the fiery eyes of a tigress. She was good—a master at playing the game, and she'd won this first round. And under the certain softness of her mouth he suddenly tasted blood. *His* blood. From that moment on, he knew he wanted to say yes, if they never spoke another word for the rest of the evening. But would she?

Dessert is served in the screened-in verandah. They sit in a circle on wicker *moras*, the men with their glasses of brandy, the women with bowls of mango ice cream, making idle chatter. Overhead, the ceiling fans whirl around, blowing streams of warm air like a desert breeze.

"More brandy?" Suresh's father asks, rising to get the snifter from the living room. "Why don't we go inside? We can finish our politics discussion."

"Indeed yes," Mr. Gupta says, taking the hint. "Before dinner, we were talking about Mrs. Gandhi's sterilization program—people getting transistor radios in exchange for vasectomies. How can that work?" Their voices fade behind the door.

Suresh's mother shakes her head at the men in disbelief. "What a topic," she says, taking Mrs. Gupta's arm. "Come, let me show you some photographs."

Both Suresh and Gita know this is their time to be together, to talk, assess and make a decision. Yet, feigning ignorance, Gita follows her mother, forcing Suresh to follow suit.

"Not you Gita," Mrs. Gupta says, thinly disguising her annoyance. "You stay there in the verandah."

Suresh's mother picks up on her cue to show the right measure of chastisement. "Suresh, show Gita to that *mora*, the big one with the rose-printed pillow. It's most comfortable," she says, smiling at Gita. "Two people can easily fit in. They could fall asleep," she fumbles, biting her tongue at the unintended suggestive turn of phrase.

Again, Suresh glimpses on Gita's face, a barely perceptible smirk at his mother's bungling words. He leads her to the *mora*. Gita sits in the middle, leaving no room for him, and begins to arrange her *sari* pleats over her knees. He sits in the one opposite, facing her, a wicker table with a bowl of red roses between them. Her face is like a map of some unknown, unexplored territory he's never been to.

When she is reasonably sure their parents are out of earshot, Gita looks up at Suresh and with no prelude or hesitation says, "We can make this quick. We both know the procedure, Suresh."

Suresh is taken aback. His other prospects had shown proper decorum by waiting for him to break the silence. Thus far, he'd always felt *he* was the chosen one; it was only *his* decision to make. And in the past, he'd played his hand well, taking his time, making mundane conversation, although he'd made his mind up long before. Now, the cards were slipping through his fingers.

"I know what *I* want," Gita adds, her eyes clear. In the stunned silence, she pauses, waiting for her words to sink in. "But first, I must ask you a question."

Suresh's heart is in his mouth. Never has he met anyone quite like her. She goes straight for the jugular. Why had she said that? For a moment, he thought she'd almost put her heart on the line, or if not her heart then certainly her mind. She'd made her decision *before* she'd had her question answered. She'd taken a chance. Or, had she? What question was she about to pop? He waits, unaccustomed to the jerky rhythms of his heart.

Gita pins her eyes on his. "How many girlfriends have you had in America?" she asks, without flinching.

"What?" The word drops from his mouth and lands with a muffled plonk on his lap.

"Girlfriends," Gita says, her voice creamy. "You know American girls. You've heard of them."

"Why are you asking such a question?" Even to Suresh's own ears, the words sound leaden. Gita lets them roll away to the corner of the room.

"Lighten up," she says, her eyes flickering with mirth. "You look like you've been caught with your hand in the cookie jar."

Suresh relaxes his tight lips. "You really had me there for a second," he says, relieved. "You sounded so serious."

"Oh, but I am," Gita says, her eyes never leaving his face. "The question is still out there floating. It's a fair question to ask, don't you think?"

"Not really," Suresh says, "it's irrelevant. I wouldn't think to ask you something like that."

"Of course you wouldn't. Because you know the answer. I live here in India. My father would fry me in boiling oil if I slept with anyone before marriage."

Suresh swallows hard, and still the words stick in his throat, grazing the inner lining raw. He rolls his tongue to the back of his mouth and tastes blood. Thick and slightly basic. He wishes his mother had left some sweet iced tea in a jug for them.

"Gita, this conversation is not. . ."

"Not appropriate, yes, yes." Gita completes his thoughts. "I know. We, Indian girls shouldn't ask such questions, even if they burn holes in our hearts. I mean, you could have a girlfriend even as we speak, someone you promised to marry—an American girl who is waiting there for you. The same way I will be waiting here when you go back to America. Until the arrangements are made, perhaps even *after* we are married. My best friend's husband lives in America and has left *her* here with his family till he finishes medical school. Why do you think that is?"

Suresh winces. "I don't know," he says, "it's a weird arrangement."

"We think we know. But she dare not ask him. And *I* shouldn't ask either. I should believe you have come here honorably."

"Okay," Suresh says, "Okay, I admit I've had, maybe three serious relationships through my medical school years. But, they didn't work out."

"You never intended for them to work out," Gita says. "You knew you would be coming home to pick a real wife. Then, you would go back to play for a while longer."

"That's not true," Suresh burst out, then stopped abruptly. He wiped his forehead with the back of his hand and measured out his words like they were alphabetical grains, one at a time. "I will not lie to you. Yes, I am—was seeing someone, until I came home, here—until today—until I met you."

"Her name?" Gita asks. Suresh looks nonplussed. "She must have a name," Gita says.

"Amy. Amy Rogers."

"Do you love her? Were you planning to marry her?"

"No, I—I'm," Suresh stutters, miserably. "That was never my plan."

Through the screened-in verandah, his eyes wander out into the garden to where a piece of paper is churning, caught in a vortex of air. The wind picks it up, lifting it a little higher, till it sails off and gets stuck in the jasmine bush at the end of the driveway. He watches it flutter, trying to break free, even as big drops of rain plop and hold it down. Gita's eyes follow his, watching the rain-drops fall, spreading in little iridescent circles, where traces of bicycle grease or car oil must have spilled on the cement.

Suresh glances at Gita. A part of him wants to rise and walk out of the room, out of her life, back to where he came from. Should he say "It was a pleasure meeting you," or, "Enjoy your day," or "Take care?" Any one of those nice, pat, parting phrases so common among acquaintances in America. After all, that's all she is—an acquaintance, he'll likely never see again. He wonders what she'd do. Would she come back with a sharp retort? Would it humiliate her? Would she simply stand up and walk away? And go on to another interview? Is she tired of playing the game? Or has she just begun?

For a moment he wants to do just that, so he can watch her make the next move. But dare he? What if there was a sliver of a chance? A silver-dotted lining? What if she *might* accept him, now that the air was clean? Could he risk throwing it all away? Unbidden, he feels the stirrings of a new excitement—mental and sexual that he's never experienced before.

With Gita, he *couldn't* imagine the future. There would be no head-nodding wife with a string of yelping kids. There would be no homemaker forcing him to eat coconut chutney with home-made *samosas*. Perhaps, she'd specialize in a different medical dis-cipline than his, and they'd never work together, not even in the same town. Or, maybe they would end up in same hospital. It was impossible to predict. With her, his life lay before him, unmarked like driven snow.

Gita looks up at him with her beautiful, implacable eyes. "Well?" she asks. "I am still waiting for your answer."

"Gita, I've told you the truth."

"I know," she says, a little smile playing on her lips. "And I told you that I know what *I* want. So, what do *you* want?"

Suresh hesitates, still unsure of where she is heading. His heart beats so fast and loud, he is certain she can hear it thudding.

"Oh, for God's sake," she says, laughing at him. "I'm going to say *yes*. And what about you?"

Suresh feels his heart thumping. He cannot fathom why he is so irresistibly drawn to this woman, nor does he care to know. For a moment, he looks deeply into her eyes. Then, bending forward, he pulls a long-stemmed rose from the bowl and carefully begins to snap off the thorns, slowly, one by one, aware that he is making a decision—a commitment, and aware that she is watching him do it. And when the rose stem is stripped bare, he hands it to her, watching her move her fingers up the smooth stem and close her palm around the blood-red petals.

III

"WOMAN, thou hast encircled the world's heart with
the depth of thy tears as the sea has the earth."
-Rabindranath Tagore

TOUCH THE MOON

Shanti strides up the well-trodden path to Mrs. Seth's house, her *chappals* flapping against her heels under her *sari* pleats.

"Ma wait," she hears Jaya's peevish call, but she doesn't stop, doesn't even turn her head. Quickening her pace, she skirts a scrawny white cow that has ambled into the middle of the road lulled by a tinkling bell around its neck. Shanti steps into the gully, side-stepping a pile of dung, then climbs back out onto the dirt road leading to Mrs. Seth's bungalow. Her daughter's voice fades away.

What more can she do? Shanti thinks. She wakes up at five every morning, says her prayers, and saunters down to the well where she is always first in line. Behind her, other village women wait, chewing on *Neem* twigs, swishing the antiseptic spittle in their mouths. Quickly, she slips the rope over the neck of a copper vessel and lowers it—down, down, over the pulley, until she hears a dull splash, gurgling, and then she heaves it up, loosens the noose and cuffs a second one. Two to a person, the women have agreed, because that's all there's time for before they scatter—some to fields, others to steel mills, most carrying basins of gravel or cement on their heads at the Palghat construction site where a government-funded building is being erected. Six stories high, with three hundred one-room flats, each with its own tiny kitchen and a tap in the wall. And at the four corners near the stairwells, communal toilets and showers on every floor. Who would get these flats, Shanti wants to know.

The government was asking for a lot of money—Rs.50, 000 as a down payment; but after that the building project would be subsidized. Rents, a modest Rs.350/month, would go toward the full purchase of the flat. It would take many years; Shanti didn't mind that, but first, who has Rs.50, 000 sitting around? And where would it come from? No doubt there'd be corruption, some palm greasing, favors exchanged under the table. The local prostitutes would fare well; even get their first choice, she thinks bitterly. Their rich "uncles" would see to that.

Up ahead the sun is peeping through groves of mango trees, mynas chattering, squirrels skittering about. She has to find a way, she thinks; she just has to. She wants one of those flats so bad she can taste it. If only she could move out of that pathetic place she's been calling home ever since the girls were born, where the floorings aren't tiled or even cemented. Not that she minds dung floors. Spread in layers, mixed with finely cut straw and lime, they make a nice, firm surface that must be resurfaced during the monsoons, but is otherwise compact, clean and odorless, unlike what the rich people think. And though her cinder block walls were not whitewashed, they were not constructed of cardboard and plastic sheets either, like the huts of city slums. There, people lived in joined-up hovels sharing walls and doors made of rags and burlap, and roofs of remnant tin and aluminum scraps, or stolen sheets of corrugated metal—huts so close together, there was barely any space in the alley for a bullock cart to pass through. There were no wells near by, no clean water, and always noise, lots of it, and smells upon smells, one stronger than the next. People urinated in gutters, even women squatted in public, she'd heard, though they made little tents with their *sari* skirts.

Shanti knows all this and is deeply grateful for her fortune, here, where the Missionary Sisters have opened a school and a medical dispensary for the villagers. They come in droves, even from neighboring villages, the line stretching around the convent building, way past the water well. Sometimes, folding tables are set up under the generous shade of the banyan tree on the convent grounds. Food and medicine is dispensed in an orderly fashion, one package per family. The Sisters keep a log in a black book marking off names and dates, so that people don't cheat and dip twice in the depleting coffers. Yes, Shanti thinks, life here is good. There is no denying it. How foolish can she be to think otherwise?

Still time was fleeting. Fourteen monsoons had come and gone for Seema, seventeen for Jaya, and still no one had accepted a marriage proposal for either girl. *Aiy*, I was already a mother at Jaya's age, Shanti thinks, hurrying. A scrawny dog follows her, yapping at her heels.

Jaya is older and prettier. Well not exactly pretty, but not as plain as Seema, Shanti thinks. Jaya is taller, slender, her hair thick and wavy like her father's, her eyes large and still, speaking a language of their own. There is an uncommon grace about her, Shanti thinks, something that might help to lighten the dowry chest. In contrast, Seema is her dark child—dark skinned, dark eyed and slow, dreaming in worlds she seems to create from the changing shape of clouds. Often she would forget to go to class, and sit on the wooden swing on the playground lost in thought. The Sisters at Holy Cross School had warned Shanti. They had coaxed, threatened, punished, even made Seema write "I will not daydream" one hundred and fifty times.

Well, Shanti muses, at least she doesn't pay for Seema's schooling. One good thing about foreign missionaries, they don't charge for anything—medicines, milk powder, cooking oil, soap, books, paper, or pencils. Shanti had seen cartons of goods arrive in lorries, gifts from the American people, she was told. God bless these generous people, Shanti thinks, each time she stocks the shelf above the water chatty. Where would she be without them? And where would she be without these sweet women who dressed like crows and lived in a house with no men?

Still, she can't help but worry about her girls. Finding a husband for Seema would be a job fit for the Gods. A miracle! Even if she could come up with a nice, fat dowry. That's why Jaya had been calling out to her earlier. Shanti knew what her daughter wanted so desperately. Again, this morning, as in mornings past, Jaya would beg for permission to leave home, to go to the city where she could find work. Again, she'd promise to send money home for Seema's future.

Shanti thinks about all this as she reaches Mrs. Seth's porch. In the verandah, Raja, the big Alsatian dog pricks up his ears as she nears. Patting his head, she slips her *chappals* off at the door and tiptoes into the kitchen, hurrying to light the new stove. Thank God for these modern, rich-people gadgets with no pumps to prime, no kerosene to fill. Just turn the knob, strike a match and poof! A blue flame burns like a flower. Shanti sets a kettle on for tea, then reaches for the sack of wheat flour. She begins mixing the flour with salt and water, kneading the dough, her mind straying far back.

She'd first come to this village with her husband when he'd found work building the main road. Shanti had found work with the Sisters. Each morning she'd go to the bazaar for fresh produce. She'd strike good bargains with vendors; she knew how to twist her mouth, shake her head, walk away if the price wasn't good; she sensed when they'd relent and call her back. Carefully, she picked the best potatoes, the firmest eggplants, the leanest cuts of beef. Once a week she took ration supplies of wheat and millet to the mill to be stone-ground. Shanti was grateful for the work especially since she was pregnant again. The Sisters had let her keep two-year-old Jaya with her during her chores. Sometimes, they even gave the child Glucose biscuits and a warm cup of cocoa milk.

Rich, influential people, fleeing the city's grime and pollution had started moving west, building homes with amazing speed unlike the government's lethargic building projects. When the Seths moved into the big house at the top of the hill, Mrs. Seth began looking for a servant—a cleaning woman who could also cook. She disliked the local villager-types, who eyed her furnishings with open-mouthed curiosity and even gawked at her red lips and fingernails. Shanti smiles recalling Mrs. Seth's decision to contact the missionaries for a reference.

"It was destiny," she told Shanti. "The Sisters spoke so highly of you; they said you were honest and clean, but they were unwilling to part with you. So, I asked them what they paid you," Mrs. Seth loved to re-tell the story. "Then I doubled it."

Shanti had seen this as a stroke of luck. Running errands, dragging two children around was difficult. She wanted a defined work routine in one location. The Seths had a beautiful home— mosaic tile floorings, carpets that felt like compressed clouds; if she kept the girls somewhat confined, they could live in rich-people comfort, at least during the day, the kind of comfort that would never be hers. Why then, is she apprehensive after so many years, she asks herself? She had thought this plan through; it wasn't an impulsive craving.

Suddenly, something soft brushes against her knees. Shanti looks down. "Oh, Anil *beta*. It's you," she says. "Just one minute, son." She hadn't seen the Seth's five-year-old boy enter the kitchen. The boy whimpers, wiping his nose to her *sari* pleats.

"One minute son," Shanti repeats. Quickly, she rolls out the last ball of dough, closes the small earthen pot of salt, folds the sack of flour and dusts her hands before picking him up. He rais-es his arms and nestles like a duckling. Shanti settles him com-fortably on her hip in the crook of her arm, his head cushioned on her breast as if he were her own—the son she doesn't have, a boy she'd ached and prayed for, whose absence in the end had cost her the man she once loved. She tries not to think about it, but like cobwebs, they cling to her heart. If God had smiled on her, would her husband have left her for a woman who would give him a boy? She ponders the question again, as she has so many times, over and over, concentric circles of misgivings. So many years alone! So many years of sorrow! Not just for her, but for her girls too. Never before or after had Shanti seen them weep so bitterly—except on the day their father left.

By noon, Shanti has finished washing the clothes—pretty lace bras, vests, underwear, Anil's little outfits. Thank God, the big things—*saris*, sheets and towels, went to the local washerman, or her arms would snap. God knows, grinding spices, preparing the day's meal and cleaning the house was plenty enough. But today was going slow—slow because she couldn't get the Rs.50, 000 out of her head. Desperately, she wanted a decent place to live, something to confer status on her girls, something with which to approach suitors and avenge the disgrace of abandonment by their father.

She knew Mrs. Seth had a wad of money stashed in the inner compartment of the *Godrej* steel cupboard. She'd seen it once when Mrs. Seth opened the safe to withdraw a gold bangle. She was no thief; she would ask her for a loan. But how? What if Mrs. Seth said no? Worse, what if she got angry and fired her? What then? Shanti hesitated. Could she take such a big chance? "Never borrow money," her mother had often said, but now as she remembers, her heart aches. She wants a flat on the sixth floor overlooking paddy fields so she'll be close to the birds, so she can touch the moon. She doesn't mind climbing steps; she's still supple from swabbing the floor, up and down, up and down, on her knees, changing the water in the bucket, rinsing the rag.

"Three waters for the living room," Mrs. Seth insists, "and reach under the cupboard. Use a hangar, wrap the rag around it and bend forward as far as your arm stretches."

Shanti had listened all these years; surely then, Mrs. Seth would understand if she explained why she needed the money. She could cut her salary in half each month till the debt was repaid. Yes, she'd like the sixth floor please, even if the water often trickled when the pump broke. Already Shanti could feel the breeze blowing through her hair in the tiny verandah.

Today is Tuesday, Mrs. Seth's busy day, Shanti thinks, laying Anil down on a quilt. The boy's eyes flicker open; she makes soft, soothing sounds and rubs his back. She'd best wait until the afternoon when Mrs. Seth returns from her Lion's Club meeting in the city. Ever since trade barriers were lifted, foreign people were pouring in like the monsoons, setting up companies and clubs, flooding the city with fancy stuff. Mrs. Seth often came back with samples—soft, high heeled, leather shoes in colors that weren't shoe-colors at all, like yellow or coriander-green, even tomato-red. Sometimes, she wore fake, long nails glued over her own, which didn't chip or come loose even in the bathtub. The refrigerator was stocked with Coca Cola and Pepsi, and bottled American Spring Water, not just Thums Up and Limca. Mrs. Seth said this exchange was a good thing; it would boost the economy, which meant more money would flow into the country, but where would it go? Shanti wonders about this, seeing nothing filtering her way. But if Mrs. Seth was a beneficiary, maybe it would increase her chances of a loan. Maybe that's how it's supposed to work, Shanti thinks. Her spirits lift. Yes, she would wait till Mrs. Seth unpacked her shopping bags and enjoyed a cup of Darjeeling tea.

Shanti had learned patience and strategy from her mother when she was a young girl. Sprawled in the verandah of their one-room house, she'd learned to catch houseflies. The houseflies were almost as big as beetles with black, oval bodies and purple-tinted gossamer wings. Not only did they make you cross-eyed buzzing around your head, but they stung too. Sharp, needlepoint pricks that itched and left a red cheroot on the skin. The swelling didn't go down till the next dawn.

Shanti watched her mother's gentle actions. Mixing a cup of wheat flour in water, she'd cook it over a low flame, stirring, stirring, till it boiled and thickened to a glutinous slurry. And when it was just right, she spread it evenly on sheaves of old, folded newspaper and drizzled pure honey over it in concentric circles like a conch shell. With the end of a broomstick she drew fine gold lines from the center to the edge of the paper, making a sweet spider's web. She set the pasty sheaves in strategic places—near her husband's feet and head, even on his chest and lap, so that he could snooze like a king.

Shanti would watch the houseflies. They buzzed over her father viciously, circled, and then landed on the honey-wheat tarmac. They struggled, and the more they struggled, the deeper their jointed legs stuck and sunk in. If only they'd thrust upward without wriggling—just one great anti-gravitational heave, they'd be free. Only once did she witness a fly do just that, and he left a pair of legs behind, legs he didn't need.

It is nearing sundown when Shanti starts back down the well-trodden path to her home. The scrawny white cow has squatted in the middle of the road, dozing, now and then jerking its head to shake off buzzing flies. In the mango groves, the mynas have stopped twittering, calmed by the twilight. Shanti walks slowly past rice fields, kicking stray pebbles, eyes stinging from disappointment, her heart cold and quiet. She pulls her *sari* tight about her shoulders, thinking.

Thinking about Mrs. Seth's face that afternoon when she'd finally got up the nerve to ask her about the money, the way she'd nodded her head but averted her eyes, the way a chill had finally crept into her voice and frozen the words that Shanti had hoped not to hear. Mrs. Seth had asked few questions. Shanti had stood there kneading her fingers in the folds of her sari, describing the little flat in the Palghat tenements with a tap in the kitchen wall and a bathroom at the end of a lit hallway. She had confessed that she was worried about her girls. They had more than come of age; if they got too old, no one would want them.

But Shanti could tell from Mrs. Seth's clenched jaw and stony silence that she was preoccupied; at times she wasn't even sure Mrs. Seth was listening. She sat there in a chair, a sadness rising from her skin, gazing out the window at the plump yellow bunch-es of plantains nestled under tall leaves. On the wall below, a baby lizard crept up a large pot of geraniums basking in the afternoon sunshine. From time to time, Shanti saw Mrs. Seth shift in her seat, pulling her thoughts back into the room but they kept slipping away. When Shanti got to the part about the loan, the air grew cool.

Well, Shanti thinks, at least, Mrs. Seth didn't get angry. At least she had allowed her to finish her story, her daydream. Perhaps, this hadn't been a good day to bring it up; perhaps she shouldn't have asked at all. For all the world, she now wishes she hadn't. She kicks a pebble, thinking—about her girls, about Jaya, and if perhaps, she should relent—let her go find her fortune in the city after all.

Shanti sighs deeply and looks up at orange tinted clouds in the evening sky. Oddly, she wonders if Seema could have foretold this day of broken dreams.

DEEP WELLS

The neon sign at the street corner read "Miraj Bar," but it served good food as well. Diagonally across was the imposing Gateway to India archway, its wide promenade strewn with hawkers and peddlers, moviegoers, foreigners, tourists and lovers strolling along the Arabian Sea. Right away Jaya pegged him for an American. She'd seen his type before—young, cocky, clean-shaven, smooth as molten tar, reeking of Calvin Klein aftershave. He stood in the door way for a minute, taking in the scene—white skinned Englishmen with crisp, cryptic accents, plates of fish and chips and beer foaming from tall, chalice-like glasses; brown-skinned Arab men, their mouths reddened from gorging on chunks of curried chicken. Ice cubes clinked in glasses of whiskey. Loud, raucous laughter rose above the piped in, lovesick songs from the latest Indian movies. He sauntered over to a table in a quieter corner of the dimly lit bar and pulled out a pack of Marlboros. Quickly, she walked over to the table.

"What'll you have, Sir?"

The man dropped his Ronson lighter in his topcoat pocket and looked up.

"Oh, Scotch, please. On the rocks," he said.

"Yes Sir," Jaya said, turning away slowly, feeling his eyes linger on the curve of her buttocks as surely as if he'd touched them. She returned promptly with his order. "Anything else?" she asked, sweetly.

"Uh, nothing thanks," the American said, then changed his mind. "Nuts, potato chips, any kind of munchies."

"Salted peanuts?"

"Love salted peanuts," he grinned. "Sure do."

She refilled his glass twice and watched him drain it in a half-hour. He beckoned to her for a third refill. "You've been working here a long time?"

"Two years," she said.

"Got any plans after work? What time you get off?" Jaya lowered her eyes. "What's the matter, sugar?"

"I'm not available, Sir," Jaya said.

The man gulped his drink down and pushed back his chair. "Figures," he muttered, laying down a meager tip, "the good ones are all taken."

Jaya stared at his receding back, ashamed and oddly hurt. Men desired her, she could tell, from the moment they laid eyes on her. Like hawks, they spotted her even from afar. And why not? Her skin was brown like *jaggery* distilled from sugarcane juice, her body slender and ripe. But it was her eyes—those windows to her soul more than her breasts and full lips that held a magnetic force as natural and powerful as monsoon gales; and all Jaya had wanted was to blow with the winds out to sea, past the horizon. "Finding a rich man was no problem," Jaya once read in some glossy, throw-a-way magazine. Rich men who snorted and panted like thirsty dogs, then left to pee in the alley came cheap, but to find one who'd stay awhile, you'd have to hook a lonely man, driven from his wife's heart, not from between her legs. "Lonely men always returned," she'd read. All you had to do was keep your mouth shut and listen. Really listen. Let him curse his boss, the traffic, the new tax laws. Let him tell you his worries about money, children, his diabetic, overweight wife, the senile mother he rarely visited. You didn't even have to understand— just nod and hum, shake your head and agree with everything, even if you disagreed. And always behave like a lady, she'd read. Not cheap, not coarse like unpolished rice flour. You eat with your mouth closed and take small sips, not gulps, even if you loved the taste. To fly with the rich, you had to be a real lady.

Yes, Jaya knew she could do all that. God may not have given her money, but He had given her beauty and good sense, and who, besides models and movie stars, had it all? Yes, she could pout her lips like an unopened rosebud, or smile like a flaming *gulmohur* blossom; she'd practiced smiling in the mirror many times before.

At home, beyond the hills on the horizon, she'd seen wriggling funnels of black smoke oozing into clean blue skies. That's where the famous American companies were—Coca-Cola, Baskin Robbins, Levi-Strauss. That's where prosperous, white-skinned Americans in shiny cars lived, dipping in and out of potholes, honking, scattering half-deaf bony dogs and gawking, pot-bellied children back into narrow alleys. That's where she'd seen women with indigo-blue eyes and hair the color of rice husks. Once in her village, Jaya had seen a lady with red lips and toenails peeping from transparent socks. Jaya had wanted to ask her if it was true—did American servants drive cars and wear gloves to

174

clean bathrooms? Were soaps really liquid—pearly and sweet scented?

Jaya had begged her mother, Shanti, to let her come to Bombay city. There was nothing there in the village, just the unforgiving cracked earth, parched dry and thirsty. Each day, the heat rose from under her feet, stinging her face and arms. Not even the wind blowing through water-drenched jute curtains could cool the hot, dry air. She would take the bus into the city. She would find work and send money home to help with Seema, her younger sister, on whom God had forgotten to smile. Seema was plain—no almond eyes or pomegranate lips, and worse, she had "a loose screw," her teacher had complained, wiggling an index finger at her temple. A touch of stupidity like a pretty birthmark was attractive in girls; it made men feel superior, the teacher said, but Seema's were like leopard spots. And she was strange too, the way she disappeared from dawn to dusk, hiding in trees, staring at clouds, insisting she could foretell her fortune from their shapes. Her father had whipped her soundly calling her a witch, but she'd remained dry eyed until he left, as if she'd always known he would.

Jaya had asked her mother why. Why had he left? She was nearly ten years old before she learned the truth, the whole story. Two in a row, two girls, he'd screamed at Shanti, and the second so ugly, it probably wasn't his. Where was the son she'd promised, hah? Where? He'd demanded an answer. Shanti was bewildered. She'd done everything a woman with child should do—*pujas* to the goddess of fertility, fasts to purify her soul, alms to beggars—and still no luck.

"Husband, please—wait, don't go," Shanti had begged respectfully, lowering her eyes, not speaking his name. There he'd stood in the verandah of their little two-room house, sweat clinging to his skin like oil, face blazing with cheap liquor. It was all her fault, making girl-babies one after the other. And now, she had stopped bearing children altogether. Why? Shanti didn't know; she too had wanted a son, but the gods were angry; they had turned their face away from her.

"I'll try, I promise," she'd pleaded.

But he had tottered out the door to find another woman, one that would bear him a son. Jaya recalled her mother's words then, as she would do in years to come, again and again. "Your father believed girls are like deep wells of sorrow into which you throw hard earned coins," Shanti said. "A little splash, a wedge of light glinting, and the money sinks, leaving only a ripple. Only a sting of metal on water."

At last Jaya had convinced her mother. "You come home for *Divali*," Shanti called, her eyes welling with tears as she waved to her daughter in the overcrowded bus. Nearby, a woman held a wriggling, bawling baby; another clutched her knees and whimpered as the bus jolted forward. Jaya bent, picked up the little girl and set her down on some piled luggage beside her. Brightened by the view from on high, the child too waved back at Shanti. By the next morning Jaya would be in the city of Bombay. In the lining of her bodice, she felt the little wad, five twenty-rupee notes rolled up, that her mother had sewn for safety.

The monsoons had come roaring in on cue washing the city clean. Well over a year had passed since Jaya's arrival; a year in which she'd finally found work in a bar, learned the names of wines, beers, drinks with little rainbow-colored umbrellas and floating olives, a year in which she'd steeled herself to become a woman. It was good money—money she sent home every month, and it only hurt that first time with Mr. Montgomery, the American, who was almost as old as her father would have been—fiftyish, graying at the temples. She remembered how shocked he'd been when she didn't know what to do. Shocked and excited, like those alley dogs she'd seen skulking by the iron gate, sniffing at garbage dumps, lifting their legs to urinate a little here, a little there, climbing atop each other, slipping off, climbing again. She would throw stones till the animals yelped and limped off, subdued.

But Mr. Montgomery was kind and Jaya had grown accustomed to him. He was *her* American, who sat at her table whenever he flew into town, then kept her at the Ashoka Hotel for three or four days, until a jumbo jet took him away to America or Germany or Japan. Often, he brought back gifts—silken lace nightgowns, bird-like bottles of perfume nesting in satin boxes, a silver clasp for her hair. He was the lonely man she'd caught and kept, the one whose feet she pressed and thighs she kissed, who ordered room service—anything she wanted: thick slabs of cheese, fruit compotes, wine, chocolates; and she could lie in creamy, scented bathtubs with gold tinted taps and liquid soaps. He even called her his "mistress," a word Jaya loved because it meant he respected her—like "*Memsahib*," the word her mother used to address Mrs. Seth, the lady for whom she cooked and cleaned back home in the village. Of course, it was a little confusing, since here it was *she*, Jaya, who was the *Memsahib*, the mistress.

Perhaps that explained why she'd been so hurt the last time he'd left for America. He was going home for his daughter, Lillie's wedding, and he hadn't done any shopping for his wife, or his girls.

"Rose is an artsy craftsy type," he'd said, handing her a stack of rupees. "Go down to the Crown Emporium and buy her a batik

177

print, or something embroidered."

"A tie-dye *sari?*" Jaya asked.

"Hmm, maybe," Mr. Montgomery said, "But I want a *sari* for my wife, too. And get a silver filigree necklace for Lillie, like the one I gave you. Lillie loves jewelry."

"What's her favorite color?" Jaya asked.

"What? Who?" Mr. Montgomery paused, his brow furrowed.

"Your wife, Sir," Jaya said. "You want a *sari* for her, right?"

"Beats me," he'd said. I think its green—no wait, that's not it, that's Lillie's color. Oh hell, I don't know. What's the difference, anyway?"

"Sir, the difference is she'll *like* her favorite color," Jaya said. "Sometimes when people…"

Mr. Montgomery chuckled. "My sweet little Jaya," he said, "It's a rhetorical question. You're not supposed to answer that."

Jaya bent down to straighten her sandal straps, so Mr. Montgomery wouldn't see her face. She hated it when he laughed at her like that. She rushed down the elevator and hailed a taxi. Crown Emporium was across the fly bridge and she wanted to get there before it closed. Mr. Montgomery had asked her not to waste time standing in those snaking bus queues, or risk her life dangling from the steps of speeding double-decker buses. As she sat in the cab, she tried to remember what Mrs. Montgomery looked like. If her eyes were blue, she'd look at blue *saris*—sky blue or midnight blue, or even an ocean blue-green to light up her eyes. If her eyes were brown, maybe a cocoa or rust colored *sari*. She tried to recreate the photograph Mr. Montgomery had once shown her. There they were, the three of them—Mrs. Montgomery, Rose and Lillie standing at the beach, arms linked, laughing, the wind rushing in their hair. Their faces were turned up against the blue backdrop of sea and a cinnamon-tinted sky.

The wind carried the sound of their laughter. Mrs. Montgomery wore a sleek, black one-piece bathing suit. Her breasts and thighs were firm, but her face showed the etchings of time. Rose and Lillie wore two-piece bikinis as gracefully as they wore their names. Rose's skin had a rosy glow like the sunset behind her; Lillie's was paler, like moonlight. Jaya knew that Mr. Montgomery adored his daughters, though he seldom spoke of them to her. She could tell from his eyes, the way he gazed at the picture, then tucked it back under the plastic in his wallet. And of course, he loved his wife too. Once when he was busy, he called the lady at the gift shop and asked her to gift wrap a brooch and clip-on earrings. Another time he'd sent her a *sari* for a "Halloween party." He explained that it was a costume party where people wore masks and dressed as characters, real or make-believe. Jaya wondered who Mrs. Montgomery had pretended to be in the lovely blue silk *sari*, dotted with silver stars, which had reminded Jaya of a starry night.

Jaya noticed that Mr. Montgomery grew pensive, almost sad, whenever he spoke of his wife. He said she liked to read mystery books at night; he liked to watch ball games on TV. No, not cricket, he explained, but another fast paced one called football, which was a lot like soccer here, but it was no fun watching the game alone. So he often stayed out with his friends at the club especially on Monday nights; by the time he got back, she'd be asleep, her face to the wall. Couldn't he gently wake her, Jaya wondered?

"Heavens, no," Mr. Montgomery had laughed. "We're way past that stage. Time and distance will do that."

Jaya didn't quite follow. She'd been away from home too, and if anything, had grown even fonder of her village. She missed the sounds of morning—cocks crowing, buckets clanging, the gurgle of well water being emptied from copper vessels into earthen

179

water pots. She missed the mellow sounds of village voices, women calling each other, talking softly. City voices were differ-ent—sharper, jagged edged. Although she had no regrets, time and distance, if anything, had had a reverse effect on her.

"You're much too young to measure time," Mr. Montgomery had said, sadly. "You have to live long enough to build regret."

Jaya returned from her shopping spree with an armload of gifts for Mr. Montgomery's wife and daughters. That night, she wore her lime-green *salwar khameez* and twisted her hair into a soft 8-shaped coil at the nape of her neck. He always wanted her to look nice; it was part of her job, he said. At dinner, he explained how Lillie would wear a long white gown, how he would walk her down the aisle in Church.

"White?" Jaya was shocked. "Not red?"

"Good grief, no," Mr. Montgomery replied. "Her bridesmaids will wear color, but Lillie will wear a white veil and..."

"Like Mother Teresa?" Jaya interrupted.

"Hell no." Mr. Montgomery roared with laughter. "You haven't seen a wedding party, have you?"

"No Sir."

There he was, laughing at her again. "I'll bring pictures," he said, "I'll show you. Oh, it's quite an event. Costs an arm and a leg too."

"How much dowry for Lillie?" Jaya asked.

Mr. Montgomery laughed again. "Dowry? No dowry. What do you think? I'm selling my daughter?"

That confused Jaya. If he were selling his daughter, he'd be receiving money, not paying it. "Dowry is not selling, Sir. It's just part of an agreement."

"There's no agreement. Lillie chose her own husband. I

haven't even met him yet. I'll probably see him for the first time at the rehearsal dinner."

Jaya had wanted to ask what they were rehearsing, but she was afraid Mr. Montgomery would laugh at her again.

Jaya tried not to dwell on her relationship with Mr. Montgomery. She'd left her home for a chance to earn money—it was that simple. Only then would there be hope for her and her family. Until she'd met Mr. Montgomery, she'd never seen foreign money—didn't even know the names. But Mr. Montgomery, who traveled to all parts of the world, showed her liras from Italy, marks from Germany, pounds from England. And of course, the beautiful dollar—the paper that changed her life.

She remembered that night well. The monsoons were about to break. Outside, the coconut palms were swaying like gigantic fans in the sky and the waves were huge—crashing on those great black rocks, spilling mounds of foam all over. She loved the monsoons—the way the heavens opened up and cried without shame—clean, pure, simple. She wished she could do that too. She and Mr. Montgomery had finished dinner in the hotel, and were sitting on a loveseat sofa by the window watching the approaching storm.

"Why did you leave your home, Jaya?" he'd asked, suddenly.

"Why? To make money," she'd replied.

Mr. Montgomery got quiet. Then he poured himself another drink, walked over to his closet and reached in the back of his suitcase. He returned with a big wad of green notes. "Have you ever seen this?" he asked, unfolding one. "That's a ten dollar bill with a picture of Hamilton."

"Who's Hamilton?"

"Alexander Hamilton, a great American Statesman," Mr.

Montgomery said. He loosened another note with his thumb. "And this here is Abraham Lincoln on a fiver."

"Who's he?"

"Abraham Lincoln? A great President."

"And who's on the twenty?" she'd asked.

Mr. Montgomery fanned out his money like a deck of cards and pulled one out. "Andrew Jackson, the seventh president of the United States."

She took the twenty dollar bill from his hand. "Mr. Jackson has a long pointed face," she said, turning the note over. "Oh, is this a palace? Or Harvard College, where you studied?"

Mr. Montgomery burst out laughing. "Neither," he said, "that's the White House."

"The White House?"

"Where the President of the United States lives."

"Oh, I see." She stared at the ten dollar bill. "Mr. Hamilton is a handsome man." She flipped the bill. "In God We Trust," she read. "That's very nice. So true."

Mr. Montgomery smiled. "Ever seen what a hundred looks like?" he asked, spreading the bills on the table. "That's Benjamin Franklin right there," he said, tapping his finger.

"Are *all* the bills green?" she asked.

"Yes, yes, it's all green. Not like Indian money. But the pictures on the back are different. See, this ten dollar one has the U.S. Treasury, and the hundred has Independence Hall—that's in Philadelphia."

She looked in wonder, flipping all the bills, staring at the green faces of the presidents and buildings. "God, I've never seen so much money in my whole life," she said.

"Yeah, yeah, the mighty dollar," Mr. Montgomery said, draining his glass of whiskey. "But, guess what? It's only money. It doesn't buy a lick of happiness. That's for damned sure."

He chuckled, and then suddenly, he went crazy. Grabbing handfuls of notes, he held them high above her head and dropped them on her like confetti. One went sailing over the bedpost, carried by the fan and landed on the lampshade. Some fell on her head, some on the cushion, the floor, the arm of the chair.

"Oh, oh, what are you doing Sir?" Jaya asked, scrambling to gather them up. Mr. Montgomery poured himself another drink, as she set the stack of notes on the table. "Sir, you've had enough to drink. Let me put you to bed now," she said.

"Not so fast," he said, "Come here." He pulled her down on his lap and reached for the stack of money. "So, you think Mr. Hamilton is handsome, huh?" He pulled a ten-dollar bill from the pile and tucked it in her blouse. "So, keep him as a souvenir," he said, "and get me some ice."

"Sir, you shouldn't.."

"Ice," he shouted. "And check out that pile. You can have all the Mr. Hamiltons you want."

She did. She found eleven Mr. Hamiltons and handed them to Mr. Montgomery. "Come here," he said, sitting up, drawing her between his legs. "Stand straight." She watched as he unfolded the notes, one by one, and tucked them, like little flags, into her *sari* petticoat at her waist, turning her around and around. He took his time, and when he was done, he pulled on the string, so the notes and her petticoat all dropped to the floor. "They're all yours," he said.

The next morning Mr. Montgomery sent her out for cigarettes. "Hurry. Just pick up a couple of packs. I'll get a carton later," he said.

She rushed out the door to the little *chai* and cigarette

store—a small hole-in-the-wall kind of place with a room in the back, where sweet milky tea was brewed and brought out in small cups to customers.

"Two packs of Marlboros, please," she said, fumbling in her purse for rupees which were mixed in with the green Mr. Hamiltons. As she paid the man for the cigarettes, a ten-dollar bill fell out. The man almost pounced on it, knocking over a cup of tea.

"*Hai Bhagwan*," he burst out, "Where you get this kind of money? You got more?" Jaya told him she had some. "*Hai*," he said, "Do you know dollar give plenty rupees?" Jaya shook her head. "You can get big note?" he asked, his eyes slimy with greed. "Twenty dollar, hundred dollar? Bigger is better, easy to sell, and you get more rupees, more value."

Jaya began to understand as he explained—she could get rich if she was willing to make a deal with his "friend." She could trade dollars in the black market, the man explained. She agreed to try. "But, can I please have the cigarettes now?" she asked, afraid she'd kept Mr. Montgomery waiting too long.

"Yes, yes. But, you—uh—just listen to me," he urged, "I am in this business. If note is clean and new, it's good money."

Ever since then, Jaya asked Mr. Montgomery to pay her in dollars. She told him she wanted new notes, unfolded, uncrushed, unmarked by coffee stains. Mr. Montgomery said the currency made no difference to him. The so-called "friend," a customer at the Miraj bar, routinely exchanged her money. He brought stacks of one-hundred rupee-notes, bundled together in a dirty, half-torn handkerchief that smelled of cigarettes. Sometimes the notes were new, stapled together, ten to a pack, numbered in sequence; other times they were loose and dog-eared. Jaya had an ongoing secret arrangement. Whenever she was ready to trade, she let him know by putting a mint on his plate of *kebabs*. That meant he should meet her the next night at the Gateway to India Archway right after the bar closed. From there, they would go to the *chai* and cigarette store, where the owner, for a fee, allowed them to sit in the backroom and make their accounts.

"Good business, no?" the owner would say, winking, each time she carried away her stack of rupees, and he put his cut away.

This arrangement, Jaya thought, was good—far more lucrative than her salary and tips from Miraj Bar. She settled into a routine, serving food and drinks, but declining the lurid advances of fat Arab sheiks with hairy paunches and gold chains, not even when they offered to double the money Mr. Montgomery paid her. She wasn't greedy or cheap. She had found her rich, lonely man. She would keep him.

"You're *my* mistress," Mr. Montgomery often said, kissing her lips. "You belong to me."

And that is why her heart broke the day he returned from America after Lillie's wedding. She'd asked the owner of Miraj Bar to let her off early, so she could meet his plane. She arrived at the airport early and booked a taxi, so Mr. Montgomery would not have to wait in line. As he emerged through the glass doors, the porter behind him, the cab pulled up to the curb. Bowing low, the porter accepted a lavish tip and winked at Jaya. Filled with shame, she moved over, so Mr. Montgomery could slide in beside her.

"Ashoka Hotel," she told the taxi driver, who nodded because he knew. Jaya had already paid him to refuse other fares, while they waited for Mr. Montgomery.

"Jaya," Mr. Montgomery said, taking her in his arms. "Beautiful as ever. You are a sight for tired eyes."

Jaya pulled away gently, feeling the taxi driver's eyes on her.

185

"How are you, Sir? Did you have a good flight?"

"Uh, not bad, not bad, just the usual delays. The usual headaches. It's just such a long, long way off. Twenty two hours in a plane? Phew. "

"How was the wedding?" she asked.

"Fine," he said, "went without a hitch. Lillie was beautiful."

"And your son-in-law? You like him?"

"Oh, well enough, I guess," he said. "Didn't get much of a chance to get to know him. They went to Hawaii for their honeymoon."

"What's that?" Jaya asked.

Mr. Montgomery laughed. "A honeymoon? Oh, it's so good to be back. I'll show you later," he said.

From the way his voice turned deep, Jaya guessed. Color flooded her cheeks. It was a long ride to the hotel. The taxi eased on to the highway over miles and miles of concrete, curving around islands of palms and flowering bushes, over the bridge, and past construction sites, where more, and yet more buildings were raising their ugly heads. Everywhere you looked, there was nothing but rain-washed concrete balconies with flapping bed sheets and *saris* drying in the sun, and people walking in every direction carrying babies or baskets, riding bicycles or bullock carts, or hanging from buses. People flooding the city from villages and small towns in search of work that didn't exist. Everyone needed money. It was that simple.

In the hotel room, Mr. Montgomery relaxed in a stuffed chair and sipped his second martini. Jaya unzipped his suitcase and began to hang up his clothes. She set a vial of almond oil out on the night stand for his massage and turned the bed covers down.

"Leave that," he said, "you can do all that later. Come over here and sit down."

Jaya sat on the edge of the chair. "So what have you been doing while I was away?" Mr. Montgomery asked, pulling her down on his lap.

"Nothing. Just working at the bar, and then going home. My landlady came last week to inspect my apartment, and I showed her where the stairs needed repairs," Jaya said.

"And what else?" Mr. Montgomery asked, yawning.

"Mr. Miraji fired the cook. Said he caught him stealing a bottle of liquor from the cabinet. Said he'd suspected it all along."

"Does that mean I don't get those spicy French fries anymore?"

"The *chai* shop at the corner makes better ones," Jaya said. "More pepper and chili, and crispier. You want me to get you some?" she asked, rising.

Mr. Montgomery pulled her down. "No way. I want you right here beside me." He drained his glass, set it down on the table, and dropped his hand to her dangling feet. "Now, why are you wearing this tight pant?"

Jaya felt her cheeks warming. "I thought you like *salvar khameez*," she said, "and normally, you want your massage first."

"That's true," he said, "normally, I do." He brought his hand up her leg over the *salwar*–pant and under her shirt, undoing the clasp of her bra. His breath was warm on her neck as his fingers dipped to her belly button and traveled back up to her breasts, back and forth. Slowly, he pulled on the cord of her *salvar* and scooped it out from under her. It gathered in a heap around her ankles.

"So," he said, hoarsely, "did you find another lover while I was gone?"

His words went through Jaya like a dagger. She sat bolt upright. "What? Another lover? Is that what you said, Sir?"

"Yes, baby, baby-Sir, that's what I said," he crooned.

Jaya stood up, her eyes burning with anger. "Is *that* what you think of me?" she said. Quickly, she bent down, picked up her *salvar*, and pulled on the cord, hurriedly gathering the material around her waist.

"Oh, Jaya," Mr. Montgomery said, patting his lap, "come on back."

"You said I was your mistress," Jaya said, her eyes welling with tears. "I thought I was *your* mistress."

"Oh, come now, Jaya," Mr. Montgomery said, "I didn't mean…"

"No Sir," she said, "if you think I'm like that…I." Tears rolled down her face.

"Jaya, you're being too sensitive. Unreasonable really. I…"

"Unreasonable? Did you say unreasonable?" She began to sob. "Today is my sister's wedding—Seema's, my only sister. I came to Bombay for her—for my mother—for—all our sakes. You went home for your daughter's wedding, but I didn't go home for my sister's—only because you said you were coming back today. I stayed here for you—because I work for *you*. It's my job."

She turned, facing the wall, and clasped her bra back in place. "You think I'm a cheap girl? You think I do this all the time?" She picked up her purse. "You think I like—*like* doing this?" She was weeping openly now.

"Jaya, I didn't mean it that way. Please don't go," Mr. Montgomery said, coming toward her.

She turned away. "I'm sorry Sir, I must. I can't. I. . .I "

"Where are you going? You can't just leave like that." Mr. Montgomery's voice was high.

"Yes Sir, I can." she whispered, between sobs. "I have to. I need to be alone."

"I'm sorry Jaya. Oh, for God's sake…" Mr. Montgomery sputtered, as she shut the door quietly.

In the elevator, she wiped her face and smoothed her clothes
down. Walking quickly through the lobby of the Ashoka, she
grabbed the tiger-head brass handles of the massive teak door and
stepped out on to the street. Throngs of people were walking,
some purposefully to fancy restaurants or movie theatres; others
were jay walking, laughing, weaving through peddlers with carved
trinket boxes, fake ivory-inlaid jewelry, and cheap silk scarves. Still
others pointed to elegant window displays—sequined belts and
ruby red brooches, shoes, beaded purses—all spread out on black
velvet like jewels. Jaya walked in the center, in the thickest part of
the crowd, finding strange comfort there. When she reached the
bronze statue of King George, she broke away from the main road,
and turned left into a gully on to a side street. If she hurried, she
could be at her door in a half hour. The side street was far less
crowded. At the corner a beggar—an old man with sunken eyes
and X-ray arms sat cross-legged, a bowl in his lap.

"*Beti*," he said, softly, "in the name of God." His eyes locked
into Jaya's eyes. "Daughter. Have mercy."

Jaya stopped, reached into her purse and pulled out a few
rupees, her heart breaking. His words filled her up for no one had
called her "daughter" in a long time.

Jaya did not go home for *Divali* the year following Seema's wedding. The owner at Miraj Bar said business was booming. Lots of
foreigners and wealthy Indians frequented the bar. He needed her
there, and of course, Mr. Montgomery needed her too. After the
night she walked away, Mr. Montgomery came to the Miraj Bar
every evening. He sat at a table alone, eating his dinner, nursing
his drinks, and when the bar closed, he walked Jaya back to her
little apartment.

"Please, Jaya," he said, over and over. "Please come back. I was wrong. I never meant disrespect."

"Sir, no one has touched me but you," Jaya said.

"I *know* that. I should have known that," Mr. Montgomery said. "And you see, I haven't touched anyone either—just you. And my wife, a long time ago," he added, sadly.

In the end, Jaya went back to Mr. Montgomery. She believed him, and besides, she had no money to send home.

A few months later, Jaya received a letter from her mother. "Come home," she read, "we haven't seen you for almost two years! Not even when Seema was given away in marriage. And now, God has blessed us with His grace. She's with child—a boy, anyone can tell by her shape, and of course, she'll have this first child at our home. Why don't you come home too?"

Jaya read her mother's letter twice over.

Tonight, he had something important to tell her, he said. Could she get off an hour early and meet him at the Taj Mahal instead of the Ashoka? Take a taxi; don't wait for those wretched cater-pillar-like buses, he said, and tell the bellboy to put it on his bill. Jaya was wondering about these new arrangements as the black and yellow cab hummed along a narrow street, scattering cyclists and idle children left and right, past the shanties with rows and rows of mud thatched roofs, so low you had to crouch to get in, unless you were a child. Mr. Montgomery once told her that in America no one lived in such low roofed spaces; they were meant mainly for storage, tucked up near the rafters. Some people had pull-down ladders to climb in there; others had an entire "attic" room. Store what? Jaya had wondered. Past the shantytowns where everything was the color of mud, the cab droned on to a two-lane causeway flanked by fishing villages. Suddenly, an expanse of blueness arose to soothe the eye; the Arabian Sea dotted with fishing boats and white froth. Fish nets were spread wide on the rocks, silver glinting in the sunlight. Jaya looked out the window as the cab began to cross the bridge, then came to an abrupt halt. A traffic jam in full bloom became visible and audible. Cars honked and people spilled from lorries and buses to investigate the delay. It was very apparent. They were putting up a big electric sign for Coca Cola on a tall building. A lorry carrying the equipment partially blocked the only lane going north. This was no ordinary sign, Jaya thought, these coke-colored letters framed in white frosted fizz, a token of Bombay's booming, bustling economy. When the cab finally eased along and began lumbering up a fairly steep hill, Jaya breathed a sigh of relief. Way up at the top against a blue sky, she could see the laterite castle with white turrets overlooking the Arabian Sea. She felt the slightest tug on her heart. She'd never been this far from the city before.

The Taj Mahal hotel was in full view now. Jaya opened her bag and pulled out a tortoise compact that Mr. Montgomery had brought her from Japan. She squinted in the mirror and powdered her nose, then dabbed perfume behind her earlobes. In the rear view mirror, she met the cab driver's amused eyes. There was a smirk playing on his lips. She put her things away hurriedly, rustling with humiliation.

"It's not the way it looks. It's not what you think," Jaya wanted to say to him. But she looked out the window and said nothing.

Mr. Montgomery was lounging on a stuffed chair sipping scotch. A crystal decanter lay by his side. In an alcove was a dark teak bed with satin coverlets and plush pillows. By the window a table had been set, centerpiece of red roses, long stemmed glasses of chilled melon juice.

191

"Ah, Jaya," he said, rising to greet her, "I was afraid you'd never come."

"No, Sir, it was a long drive and there was a traffic jam on the bridge," she said.

She kissed him and began to undo his shoelaces as always. He had many pairs of shoes, her American, all made in Italy, with socks to match his shirts. His wife must buy them from those glittering department stores that resembled cities. Pushing her bangles up her arm, she gripped his calves, flexing his ankles, pulling gently on the ligaments and tendons of his feet. Mr. Montgomery sat back, staring at the ceiling.

"You're very quiet tonight, Sir. Is something wrong?" she asked.

"No, no, nothing," he said, absently.

Jaya pulled gently on each toe, cupped her palm around all five and tilted them, backward and forward. Grasping the heel, she gently rotated his foot clockwise, then counter clockwise, and pressed her fingers around the periphery of his foot, around his ankle bone, which jutted out slightly.

"Do you want your hot tub first?" she asked.

"No," Montgomery said, pointing. "Look, I planned a lovely dinner. I'll ring the waiter."

The waiter brought in steaming tandoori chicken, saffron rice and mint yogurt. "Would you like mango *lassi* now or later, Madam?" the waiter asked Jaya.

Jaya's face reddened. "Now please," she said. Mr. Montgomery knew how much she loved mango *lassi*. They did not speak until the waiter had left. Montgomery watched pensively as she tucked into a chicken breast.

"Jaya, did you finish school?" he asked, abruptly.

"Yes, till eighth standard," she said, "in my village at the Holy

Cross School."

"Your family lives there?" he asked.

"Only my mother and sister. My father left us."

"Why did you leave your village?"

Jaya stopped eating. Why was Mr. Montgomery plying her with questions today? "To work," she answered simply. "My mother needed money for my sister's dowry—gold bangles, *saris*, copper pots…"

"And you? What about you?" Montgomery interrupted.

"I don't want to marry," she said.

"What then? What do you want to do?"

"I work at the Miraj Bar Sir, and I work for you," she answered, simply.

Montgomery pushed away his plate and walked to the window. The sky was clear, filled with stars. He could hear the Arabian Sea pounding mercilessly against the rocks.

"You are not well?" she asked, "Shall I order mint tea? It's soothing."

He didn't reply, and when she looked again she saw there were tears in his eyes. Good God! What had got into her American? She didn't think they cried, that they would ever need to cry. They had everything that money could buy, and didn't money buy anything that anyone could ever want?

"Do you remember the first time?" he asked.

He meant *that* first time; who could ever forget that? Does anyone? Jaya cringed; it was so shameful. No one had told her what happens, not even her mother, and she hadn't seen it in those silly Hindi movies either, where girls danced around trees, teasing, tantalizing, but never kissing. Never had she imagined what came after. Mr. Montgomery's lips had tasted like burnt whisky, and his large, mottled hands felt hot as he cupped her cold breasts and squeezed her nipples.

"Come on baby," he'd said, "Don't be shy."

She'd stood still, trying to close her eyes like Julie Andrews in *The Sound of Music*. And that's when she'd felt it—stiff and hard against her thighs, the thing that everyone in her village longed to find between newborn thighs, the thing that was missing in girl-babies. Suddenly she'd begun to cry, had known instinctively what was going to happen. She'd stood there sobbing; a captured bird with wet feathers, breasts stinging from his fingers.

"My God, you really are a child," he'd said, "a real virgin, aren't you?"

And then she'd cried even harder from the shame of trying to be the woman she wasn't, from shocking and disappointing the nice American man, who would teach her, he said.

Jaya pushed her plate aside and walked into the bathroom. Uncapping a bottle of rose essence, she poured a few drops into his steaming bath. Tonight, she would massage his neck with almond oil; he seemed so weary. She was glad she'd brought her white silk nightgown with the lace bodice that he'd given her. But when they lay together, his head against her breast, he wouldn't touch her. Not that way, not this night.

Jaya fell asleep, exhausted. In her dream, she saw the silhouette of a man far in the distance walking toward her, a dark bundle on his shoulders—blankets, or a sack of wheat or corn, perhaps. Jaya squinted, shading her eyes against the glare of the sun. The man came closer, stepped in and out of the shadows, his elbow bent, one hand on the bundle. Jaya quickened her steps, running toward him. Now she could see the sandals on his feet, his worn trousers, an army green shirt ripped at the exposed shoulder, his dark pitted skin. She blinked; she knew this man, she'd seen him before. He was calling her name, beckoning, pointing to the bundle. Jaya ran faster and just as she reached, the bundle awoke and began to wail. In her father's arms was a little boy.

Jaya sat up with a start, her heart pounding. Beside her, the bed was empty, the imprint of Mr. Montgomery's head still on the pillows. She rubbed the sleep from her eyes and looked around. On the nightstand was an envelope pinned to a note.

"Jaya, my darling," she read, "I will not be coming to Bombay for a long time, perhaps never. My work here is done. You always made this old man happy—you who are no older than my daughter. I hope you find your way back to your village."

Jaya slit open the envelope. Inside, was a stack of new one hundred-dollar bills clipped together. She began to count. "One, two…." flicking her thumb and index finger. "Twenty," she gasped. Two thousand dollars! Many thousand rupees! A deep, deep sadness, a solitude, dark and heavy as monsoon clouds enveloped her. Her American had left her too. Gone.

Jaya dressed slowly, gathered her things, and tucked the money carefully in her bra, spreading the notes against her skin so they wouldn't crush. She walked across the room and stood by the window. Below, the tide was rolling in. Big waves thrashed against black rocks sending sprays of salt water over the wall on to the sidewalk. The sky was the color of ash except where the sun's first rays were starting to burn through the clouds. In another hour, the tide would recede; the sun would blaze out and dry the pavement. Far in the distance the taillights of an airplane were blinking. Closer, flying low, were sea gulls feasting on the morning's catch that the tide was bringing in. Jaya turned away and closed the door softly behind her. In the hotel lobby, the bus boy called a cab though she didn't ask for one.

"It's paid for," he explained, opening the door for her.

The village was exactly as she had left it. Parched earth craving rain, a burning wind, whirls of dust like yellow flour, cows chewing their cud, the buzz and odor of flies hovering over clods of dung. The road looped past rows and rows of tarpaulin-covered shacks lining the street like railroad tracks, past Holy Cross School covered in ivy, and beyond that, the home she'd left so long ago. She heard her sister's screams even before she rounded the culvert, before she passed the tamarind tree, well before she reached the low stone wall and pushed open the wooden gate. Smoke billowed from red coal embers, the incense crackling, the air fragrant. Running up the cracked steps, she threw open the door and stepped in, elbowing her way past women huddled together. Into the back room—and there she stopped.

Seema looked up at her sister, her face drenched in sweat. In her arms she cradled it, holding it tenderly to her breast, a sweet little baby with nothing between its legs.

BIRTHMARK

Well before he hears the postman's knock, Vipul catches a glimpse of his khaki uniform and Gandhi cap through the mango grove. Hurrying outside, he slits open the telegram feverishly, mouthing the words over and over—a simple line from his wife, Seema.

"Girl born May 9th, seven pounds. Both well."

Relief washes over him. At least Seema has had a safe delivery. As was customary, she'd gone home to her mother during the seventh month of her pregnancy. He knew there was no hospital nearby in her village, that a mid-wife would be summoned to the house when the time drew near. Other women-friends would be there too with incense sticks and offerings of flowers and sweets. There would be plenty of scented warm water. That's what Seema had told him before she left. That's how it was always done in her village.

Vipul folds the telegram announcing his daughter's birth, puts it into his pocket and walks into the kitchen. He picks a guava from the fruit bowl and bites into the green rind, crunching the seeds between his teeth. It is a moment of mixed elation. Yes, he has a child, a child of his very own. No matter if it happens to be a girl. At least he has *something*—the one thing that his older brother, Mahesh, doesn't.

Vipul cannot wait to tell his mother, Durga, the good news, but for now, he is glad the house is empty, so he can savor this auspicious moment. Durga had gone to visit her doctor in the adjoining village a few miles away. Vipul had insisted that she go. He'd even paid for a *tonga* fare; he knew she preferred the steady clip-clop of a horse carriage to the petrol and exhaust fumes of buses. He has been worried about her health, more so since his father's death two years ago. Back then, he thought she would collapse under the weight of her sorrow like an overloaded bullock cart—how she'd taken off her earrings and smashed her wrists on the tile floor beside her husband's body, shattering her multicolored glass bangles. She'd put on a plain, white, cotton *sari*, and from the parting of her hair, she'd rubbed off her *sindhur,* a bright red powder, the joyous mark of a married woman. Then she'd locked herself in her room, refusing to speak to anyone.

Unlike Mahesh, Vipul had taken charge. He'd stayed home from work that whole week. He'd stood outside her door, calling, coaxing, pleading with her to open the door, but to no avail. Finally, on a little stool in the hallway, he'd placed a stainless steel *thali* of fresh fruit, a tumbler of water, and small jagged pieces of unrefined rock-sugar to place under her tongue as an instant source of energy. On the first night, the tumbler disappeared into the room, but the fruit and sugar remained outside. A steady aroma of incense emanated from the doorjamb. On the second day, again the water disappeared; the fresh replacements of mango and coconut remained untouched. Chant-like moans rolled from under the door; Vipul couldn't tell if she was delirious or reciting incantations, perhaps to invoke his father's spirit. He'd kept calling, but there was no answer, nothing to disrupt the imploring, rhythmic words of grief.

That night, he lay awake remembering how she used to be. How he longed to hear her well-worn, martyred voice repeat the mock phrases she'd used all through his boyhood years. "What is it now son? Can't a mother get some rest?" she would say, whenever he called her, even as she dropped whatever she was doing, ready to fulfill his slightest wish for whatever it was—a savory snack, a clean towel, medicine for a real or imagined ache.

"Aiy," she would smile, pinching his cheek, "how much will you eat? Does your stomach have a hole in it?" And she'd tickle his navel, or holding his head in her palms, she'd shake it gently saying, "Your head hurts? Let me see if there's any water in it." And she'd make a babbling-brook sound with her lips as if his head held water. Or she'd purse her lips making no sound at all. "Na, na," she'd say, "Aiy, khali, it's empty. This coconut head is hollow." And she'd burst into a peal of laughter.

If only she would eat something—a plantain, pineapple, or the golden, ripe guava he'd plucked off the tree that morning. "Amma," he'd called, "taste this guava. It's so sweet."

But she'd remained behind closed doors in an eerie silence interspersed with chants. How painful those days had been, how long and slow. It was as if the earth was a broken toy that stopped every few hours and quit revolving. The sudden, unexplained death of his father was heart-wrenching enough; without his mother, Vipul feared he'd be left alone in the world with an older brother he barely knew.

But on the seventh day, Vipul recalls, a woman dressed in startling white had flung open the door and stood in a pool of twilight, a lit *diva* in her palm. Her face was drawn, her arms hung like the thin forearms of a chimp, her stomach pressed against her spine, her eyes vacant. Vipul had rushed to her side, lifted her gently in his arms and carried her into the verandah. He'd laid her against a stack of pillows on the armchair and rubbed her feet. The last rays of life-giving sun were beating in, warming her face, bringing color to her cheeks. He'd held a cup of warm turmeric milk to her lips and watched her swallow sip by sip. He'd dipped small pieces of *puris* in yogurt and fed her, as she had done for him many years ago.

After that fateful day, Vipul remembers, his mother had turned a page. Each day she'd grown stronger in body and mind as if her husband's spirit had chased away the angel of death. It was the beginning of a deep, unspoken devotion that Vipul felt for his mother, a new umbilical cord. Always, she would be the woman he most loved.

Vipul slips his feet into his sandals and closes the door softly behind him. A brisk walk before lunch will clear his head, he thinks. His mother should be home before dusk. Stepping out on to the narrow cement path, he walks past the purple bougainvillea vines draping his neighbor's wall, past the mango grove and the drab elementary school building the government had just opened. Children are running around in the compound, tossing balls, swinging from tires fastened to trees, chasing each other. Vipul watches a bevy of girls jumping rope, taking turns, counting *ek, dho, theen, char.* Overhead, dark clouds begin to gather and a wind picks up puffing up their skirts, blowing pieces of paper and dry leaves about the yard. Vipul looks up at the pewter sky. Not today, he thinks, walking on, this will blow over. It will be another week before the monsoons break in full force.

His marriage proposal had arrived on a day like today—a morning in June, a prelude to the monsoons. He'd slit open the envelope and read the letter aloud to his mother, who did not know how to read. It was brief and to the point. "My daughter, Seema," he'd read, "has attended school up to the eighth standard. She is fluent in both Hindi and English. She is about five feet tall, quite good-looking with long brown hair, excellent at cooking, cleaning and keeping house. Her father, a bricklayer, passed away when she was two years old. By God's grace, we have money, a nice dowry, put aside for her. I know you want a good girl from a good family for your youngest son. Would my daughter interest you? When can I visit?"

Vipul was breathless. True, he'd always known he wasn't as good looking, smart, tall, or anything, as Mahesh. Even as children, the difference had been clear. To their face, people called them *bada/chotah bhai*—big/small brother, but behind their backs, cruel contrasts—fat/thin, clever/stupid, manly/girlish, were whispered. Vipul had compensated with resilience, never missing class or cricket practice even when he was ill, staying away from cigarettes and cheap whiskey. He had worked long and hard. Now, at last, he too would have a wife. Durga asked him to reread the letter, slowly and clearly.

"What are you thinking, Amma?" he'd asked, when he'd finished.

"Nothing, nothing, I'm just thinking."

"But *what* are you thinking?"

She'd remained pensive. "*Quite* good-looking," she repeated, "means the girl is no beauty, but her hair must be pretty. The 'passed away' bricklayer father—well, you know what that is? It's a disguise for desertion—an expression abandoned women use—an unspoken code," she said.

"But it may be true. It is, in your case," Vipul had said, unable to stop himself.

Durga had lowered her eyes, but not before Vipul saw the expression on his mother's face. He saw the razor-sharp pang of desolation imparted only by death, the sorrow of living alone without a man to draw the ache from her body. He looked away.

But Durga had recovered quickly. "Read the line after that," she said.

"*By God's grace, we have money, a nice dowry, put aside for her.*" Vipul read. "Well now, how much have they been graced with, I wonder?" Durga muttered half to herself.

That morning, Vipul saw his mother fold the letter carefully and tuck it behind a picture of Lakshmi, the goddess of Fortune, seated on her lotus throne. For a long time she'd stood before her, praying silently. He could only guess what images floated behind her closed eyelids. He knew Mahesh's wife, Saroj, had been a disappointment. No matter how many prayers and garlands of flowers were offered at dawn and dusk to the goddess of fertility, Saroj's stomach had remained flat as a plate. At night, Vipul saw his mother feed her almonds soaked in milk and *kesar*, the slender female organ of the saffron flower. These things, she said, ripened a woman's body to receive the seed of man. But there had been no grandson. Durga had even doubled the number of almonds and prayers, insisting that Saroj eat the soaked nuts twice a day. An anger and sadness had settled in the rafters of the house as everyone had grown weary of waiting.

Now, with the letter, there was hope again. "A new daughter-in-law," she'd smiled, imagining exactly how it would be—a baby named after her beloved husband, a boy playing sticks and stones in the compound, chasing crows off the clothesline, eating peanuts and leaving the shells behind for her to clean up. He would be the smartest one in his class; he'd go to college, be a doctor or a business man some day. "Who can say?" Durga said, smiling at Vipul. "Who knows what's in our *kismet?*"

Seema hadn't taken long to conceive. Within a few months, she'd complained about feeling dizzy, and she'd lie awake at nights longing for her mother's mango chutney. Durga had been ecstatic.

"Come here," she'd say to Seema, taking her by the hand. "Stand here by the window in the light. Let me see."

She was certain it was a boy, she'd told Vipul. She could tell from the size and shape of Seema's stomach, the way it grew, the way Seema carried herself, the way the baby's head lay, facing east. She'd seen this before from the contours of other women's stomachs, and of course, her own too. Not just once, but in her case, twice, with both Vipul and Mahesh. "When a woman is with a male child, I can always tell," Durga said.

Vipul saw that his mother was treating Seema as if she was a queen. She'd buy lots of fresh fruits—bananas, chickoos, guavas, sometimes a big red apple just for her, and vegetables prepared any way she wished. No more okra or squash. No more watery *dals* or oil-fried *rotis*. Everything was delicious, cooked in *ghee*. "For my grandson," she'd say, "It will make him strong."

As Seema's belly grew, Durga had begun to try on different names for her grandson, conferring with astrologers, soothsayers, and palm readers—Pradeep, Govind, Ravinder—she would pick one depending on the day of the week and time of the boy's birth. Or, if the stars were aligned correctly, she'd like to call him Arjun, after her beloved husband, the child's grandfather.

Now, as Vipul waits for his mother's return, a knot begins to form in his stomach. He knows she'll be disappointed. But, at least he has given her a grandchild, he thinks, which is more than what his brother has done, or is likely to do anytime soon, even though he's been married for two years longer. If anything, Vipul had noticed that Saroj was more reticent, turned inward, like an unopened lotus bud. Now suddenly, he feels an odd sense of loss for this poor barren girl, his brother's wife, who will bear the brunt and blame of his own success with Seema.

Anxious to deliver his news, he wonders what is keeping his mother. Perhaps she'd stopped off to visit her sister en route. Perhaps the wheel of the *tonga* had broken. Where is she? By nightfall, the knot has hardened to stone. Skipping his evening meal, Vipul pours himself a stiff drink, slips his shoes off, and lies down. Semi-conscious, on the fringes of sleep, he is suddenly awakened by the clip-clop of a horse's hooves outside his window. The sound stops abruptly. Grabbing the telegram from his bedside table, Vipul rushes downstairs.

"*Amma*, where have you been?" he cries, hugging Durga, waving the yellow piece of paper with its perforated edges.

Durga's eyes light up. "What? A telegram? Oh, don't tell me. Oh, son," she says, "Never mind, yes tell me, tell me. I am a grandmother, no?"

With one hand she reaches for the telegram, eager to devour its contents, even though she cannot read. Vipul leans over, puts an arm about her and reads aloud.

"Girl born May 9th, seven pounds. Both of us well."

The moment lasts a thousand lifetimes. Durga's eyes cloud over, her lips set in a thin line, her feet sink into the ground. The telegram drops to the floor. Vipul turns to face his mother—this woman who had given him birth, raised him, and almost deserted him, but returned to earth that frail morning. Even in his dreams, he never imagined her reaction, a disappointment so dense that no slant of light came through. There is not a trace of joy in her eyes, only a hard coldness, the color of steel.

As the days wear on, Vipul notices there are no reference to the child. It's as if there has been no news from Seema, as if they are all still waiting. No *puja* of gratitude has been performed, no temple offerings, no shopping. Vipul says little; he is reluctant to break with tradition and interfere; it's his mother's job, and he's willing to wait. It's really hard on her, he imagines. She had desperately wished to resurrect his father. She had waited for this event, anticipated the outcome with great certainty; she needed more time to digest her disappointment. Certainly, Vipul thinks, he can give her that much. He sends his wife a carton of Alphonso mangoes, the best and tastiest variety; he knows it's her favorite fruit, and little pairs of silver bangles and anklets for his daughter. Soon her ears will be pierced, as is customary for little girls. Maybe his mother will buy her matching earrings, he thinks, when it's time.

But time is slow in coming. When Vipul finally gets up the nerve to ask her about the *puja* one afternoon as she's preparing the evening meal, she doesn't reply. In fact, Vipul isn't even certain she's heard him, although the knife in her hand suddenly flies over slivers of onions and garlic pods. On the kerosene stove plumes of steam rise from a pot of soaked beans. In a saucer are two green chilies, a skinned piece of ginger root, and an assortment of ground spices—cumin, turmeric, coriander, tamarind paste, all precisely measured out. Durga pumps the stove up and stirs the pot vigorously.

"*Amma,* did you hear me?" Vipul asks.

She nods, staring down at the sprouted beans, and when she looks up he sees her eyes are filled with tears, whether from the onions or a deep, deep sorrow, he cannot tell.

Vipul wishes now that he had left immediately to visit his wife and daughter. But at the time, the traditional forty-day waiting period hadn't seemed that long considering the steep bus fares and rigors of his clerical job. Where before he copied numbers down in rows and columns in long, blue-lined notebooks, he is now expected to draw his own charts on a machine called the computer. Where before mistakes on paper could be erased or inked out with a few pen strokes, he now has to open multiple "files," learn programs, and jump through hoops to correct just one number, and then something else gets inadvertently erased, or misplaced, as if the machine has a mind of its own. It's mind-boggling, he writes to Seema. Everything is moving too fast—faster than he can learn. Everything is being restructured, new bosses appearing from central headquarters, ordering him around, telling him to do first one thing, then another, and another, often contradicting themselves. He isn't sure to whom he should listen, which job to do first. Four months ago, the workers had been promised a raise but it was still coming. In a bullock cart, they joked, bitterly. There were stirrings of a possible strike. How could he put in for leave, or report sick now? What if he were replaced? God knows there were plenty of people, smarter and more experienced than he.

"Soon," he writes to Seema, "very soon. It won't be long now." Had she noticed that the silver bangles were engraved on the inside with the child's name? Neelam, blue water. "A pretty name," he writes.

As days pass, Vipul senses his mother is brooding deeply. In her world nothing has changed; her husband is still dead, and she has no grandson. That child in Seema's womb had been a boy, she told Vipul; she knew it; she'd felt him kick against her palm ready to fight his way out into the world. What had Seema done to cause his little penis to recede? Had she over exerted when she went home to her village? Forget to say her prayers? Did she brew the root tea she'd been given? How else could such a catastrophic error occur? Vipul knew that his mother was an expert; she had predicted the sex of many babies in their village. How on earth could she be wrong about her own grandchild? Impossible, she tells Vipul. Something must be wrong with Seema, she says.

Vipul hears his mother out. Disappointment brims in her eyes. He knows he is the cause of it, and he too, is heart broken. Perhaps, in time, in a few months, she'll feel better. He notes that she now fasts on Tuesdays, and spends most Saturdays at the temple. Both at dawn and dusk, he hears her chant, and on the family altar, sandalwood incense and oil divas burn. Fresh strings of jasmine buds are threaded and put around framed photographs of favored gods. Some day soon she'll calm down, Vipul thinks. He'll wait to tell her about his plans to bring Seema and Neelam home after *Divali*, the Festival of Lights.

Vipul awakens early, well before the pale light of morning spreads across the eastern sky. From his window he can see scarves of filmy clouds sliding as if pulled across by the invisible hand of God. There's a slight puff of breeze. In the neighboring yard, a rooster fluffs up his feathers and clucks noisily to attract three hens, who are busy scratching a rubbish pile. Turning away, Vipul hurries to bathe and get dressed for work. In less than a week, he'll leave for Seema's village, and he has still to inform his mother.

Durga is seated on the back doorstep in the kitchen, facing the yard, watching the rooster mount one hen, and then chase another. As Vipul enters the kitchen, the kettle begins to boil and hiss.

"Ah, son, you up early today?" Durga asks, rising to rinse the teapot. "Could you pass me that tin of Darjeeling?" She lowers the flame, measures out four heaping teaspoons of tea leaves into the warmed teapot and fills it with steaming water. Stirring vigorously, she replaces the cap and covers it with a warm towel as if it were a child.

"*Amma*," Vipul says, "I got up early to tell you something." The tone of his voice makes Durga stop fussing with the towel. "Next week, I want to bring Seema and Neelam home for *Divali*. I've taken leave on Tuesday."

Durga swivels on her heels. "What?" she cries, her voice high. "This year? *This Divali?* How can you think to do something like *that?*"

"Do what?" Vipul asks, taken aback. "Bring my wife and daughter home?"

His mother stares at him. "Why, haven't you noticed?" she asks.

"Notice what?"

Vipul stares back and suddenly Durga's face breaks into a huge smile. "Oh, you boys," she says, reaching across to muss up her son's hair. "I can't take it any more. Both you and Mahesh. You are quite something." She pauses, gazing at her youngest son. "Do you ever see what's right there in front of your nose? Do you always walk around like that teapot with a towel on your head?" She begins to chuckle.

"What Amma?" Vipul asks. "What is there to see?"

"What is there to see? Well, when was the last time you looked at Saroj?" Durga asks. Vipul watches his mother take two soaked almonds from a mug on the counter, slip their skins off, and fill the mug with steaming sweet turmeric milk. On a plate is a thinly sliced apple and pomegranate seeds. "Look carefully. She'll be down in a minute. This milk is for her," she says, reaching for a fragrant strand of *kesar* to lace the top. "Does that tell you anything? Does this all look familiar to you, huh?"

Vipul listens in awe. He has never seen his mother so happy except on the day she took Seema to the doctor. It was that simple. The doctor had examined Seema; yes, there was a baby in there all right; no doubt about it. His mother said it was a boy; she knew it. Now she knew it again.

As Saroj enters the kitchen, Durga hands her the mug of turmeric milk. "Drink all of it now; not just half cup," she says, gently. Saroj smiles a little, lowers her eyes and walks into the yard, holding the warm mug to her heart.

"You see?" Durga says, turning to Vipul. "Just look at Saroj. Any blind man can see. Sweet god! After all this time—I had almost given up hope. We'll have a boy to carry on our family name at last. A boy bearing the birthmark of his grandfather."

Vipul nods and stands aside, watching Saroj from the kitchen window. She is seated on a wooden bench under a flaming orange *gul-mohur* tree, sipping her milk. Her face is serene.

"So, can you wait?" Durga asks. "Just a few months more? Saroj needs peace and quiet. She is a beautiful woman, but not as strong as Seema. A new baby in the house will be disruptive. She'll wake up and cry and interrupt Saroj's sleep. The house isn't so big, after all."

Vipul's heart races inside his chest like a trapped animal. "Wait? What do you mean? How long?" he asks.

"Son," Durga says, as if she's speaking to a child. "Listen to me. A girl-baby in the house isn't good for Saroj—the aura of femaleness, the murmurs of her heart, Seema's presence—all this could change a woman's karma. Saroj must stay focused, concentrate on her baby boy, not waiver even for a second by casting eyes on a girl-child. I'm going to personally take care of her."

"When will she go to her mother's house?" Vipul asks.

Durga clears her throat. "Well, we'll see," she says. "Not as early as Seema did—maybe just a few weeks before her due date, if at all. I'm not taking any chances this time."

"And does Saroj know this?" Vipul asks, hiding the edge in his voice.

"She doesn't need to know," Durga snaps back. "Who knows how many chances we'll get? Who knows if the gods will ever smile on us again?" She takes a deep breath. "Can I please just *live* to see my grandson? After that, bring the girl-child into the house."

"Her name is Neelam," Vipul says, softly. "Blue water."

"Yes, yes, Neelam," Durga says, "I know her name. All I'm saying is wait. Wait a few months. Let good luck enter this house. Let a new generation of sons begin. Time will pass quickly. Then you can go bring your family home," she says, pausing a moment. "If you wish to," she adds, holding her son's gaze.

Vipul drops his eyes to the floor. He knows it will be a long time before he brings his wife and daughter home.

GIRL-CHILD

Jaya must make up her mind today. For several months she'd come here and stood in the shade of a lone tamarind tree watching the building grow taller. A hundred people, mostly women, had formed long queues like an undulating snake meandering from the cement pit to the work site, passing basins of sand and cement, one to the other, in a slow cadence. She'd watched the men, their hair whitened with dust, pouring and smoothing the slate gray mix with trowels and lathes. Jaya would almost fall into a trance watching their dance-like rhythms.

But now, the bamboo scaffolds, once alive with ant-like people towering toward the sky were gone. Gone too, were the large pipes and coils of thick electric cable swallowed by the earth. It had been a giant undertaking, but the bulk of the construction was over. In fact, someone had even planted the venerated Tulsi, so dear to Lord Vishnu, in the courtyard—a sure sign that people had begun to move in.

Standing there with her two-year-old niece, Neelam, in her arms, Jaya swallows a sudden wave of anger that hits her. Some four years ago, her mother, Shanti had wanted a sixth floor apartment, high up there, from where she could touch the moon, she'd said. What would it have hurt Mrs. Seth to lend them a down payment? She could have deducted it, month by month, right out of Shanti's pay. Jaya still remembers her mother's eyes—the flickering ambivalence of indecision, whether to ask or not, and then the flame of hope. In the end, it was nothing, just an illusion of gemlike brightness, the moon and all those stars growing dimmer night by night, as if the earth had moved even further away.

It is a difficult decision, one she must make alone. Should she make a down payment? She has money now, secretly earned from a life she'd left far behind in Bombay, a place to which she'll never return. Not that she has any regrets. She'd done what had to be done, and when Mr. Montgomery, her benefactor, the man to whom she had lost her virginity, left, he gave her a gift, a small fortune—$2,000 in crisp dollar bills, which she exchanged in the black market for a thick stash of rupees.

Of course, there were other options for her inheritance. She could open a small business—something like a maid service would be lucrative, she thought, especially with foreigners, who were flocking to the city like bees to a jasmine flower. Foreigners, she knew, were accustomed to their machines—dishwashers and washing machines, hair dryers, blenders, can openers, anything to save time. Here in her village, time was spent living, keeping body and soul in one piece. So, why not provide human machines? She could smell the need and taste the luscious profits it would generate.

Very gently, Jaya moves Neelam, on to her right hip. She pats the child's head, waiting for her to fall back to sleep. But the child awakens and comes alive, and points to a set of swings, a slide, and a see saw, all painted red.

"Ah, so now you're rested, and you want a ride, huh?" Jaya asks, rescuing her braid from Neelam's clenched fist. She walks toward the play area, aware that it is private property. Smiling at the workmen around, she asks, "It's okay to give the child a little ride, yes?" She knows the rules won't allow it; but it's worth a try.

A man in a red turban grins, and waves his hand. "Sure, go ahead. Who will know? Superintendent came yesterday; he won't come today."

Another man, jockeying for attention says, "For you, *sundari*, pretty lady, why not?"

Jaya settles Neelam's chunky frame in the seat curving her fingers around the links of the chain. "Hold tight," she says, but even before she begins to push, the child squeals with delight. Already her niece's cheeks are flushed like the wild roses trailing the fence. Jaya begins to push harder, then a little harder, as Neelam's joyful screams grow louder.

Jaya is reminded of her favorite poem by Robert Louis Stevenson, "The Swing," and how as a child, Sister Joan would take her class out to a sprawling old banyan tree and spread the children out among the drooping roots and branches. There, they would grasp the long hanging rope-like roots as if they were the ropes of swings, bend their knees and pretend, doggedly swaying, rising and falling in happy little waves to the rhythm of the poem. She hears their collective childish voices, especially her own—

"Up in the air and over the wall,

Till I can see so wide—"

She hears the smacking of lips, the giggles and the words "Up-p-p," and "wi-i-de" drawn out in long syllables.

"River and trees and cattle and all

Over the countryside."

Jaya joins in now, the words returning as if it were yesterday, as she pushes the swing. Her heart feels airy, light as the flitting butterflies around them.

"Till I look down on the garden green,
Down on the roof so brown—
Up in the air I go flying again,
Up in the air and down!"

"Go on, go on," Jaya calls joyfully, "Neelam, from here you'll touch the sky and the stars and the moon."

And in that instant her mind is made up.

It isn't just that their house is too small for three women and a child. It's also an aching bond that ties her to her niece, the pull of destiny as strong as gravity itself. Jaya had suffered a fate similar to Neelam's many years ago, but at least she'd seen the face of her father and known the man who'd abandoned her because she wasn't the son he'd yearned for. But Neelam's sorrow, once she learned the truth, would be far deeper and unimaginable. She would learn that her father hadn't laid eyes on her, hadn't even come to claim back his wife and baby and take them home. Even now, after all this time, Jaya feels a stab of sorrow for herself, for her niece, for all girls who are abandoned at birth. Desertion by death can, at least, be reconciled, she thinks. It can be mourned, grieved, and put to rest. But abandonment, for no other reason than your gender?

Anger starts to bubble like a dormant volcano, overpowering her profound sorrow. She pushes the swing hard, harder. When will it end—this discrimination, this hypocrisy of men who devalue women, even their own wives and daughters? And yet, their birth is the gift of their mother. And how do women blithely go about raising sons, then make outrageous dowry demands as if their sons were investments, sources of added income? How can men leave daughters to be raised by mothers—these girls, who in turn, become the mother of sons? It is a vicious circle of knots tied by tradition and superstition and economics and ignorance and. . .

Jaya doesn't see it coming, nor does she hear Neelam's cry of terror. She's been pushing the swing to the beat of her thoughts, the pulse of injustices carried in her heart for too long, a heart that is pounding. When Neelam falls, her heart stops. Sorrow gushes out; panic fills the spaces. It happens in that split second between two thoughts, a moment she wishes to take back, just one step, and relive again. Rewrite the line, change the story, change the ending. She hears a stunned silence on the last note of Neelam's scream. This is not how it's supposed to end.

Jaya grabs the chains of the empty swing, jerks it to a stop, and runs straight toward the heap that has been flung by some unnamed force. Panting, she kneels beside the child, and begins to weep. Neelam lies unconscious in a pile, her dress bunched up and brown with dirt. There is a red gash near her temple, a bruised knee, an arm scraped in long furrows from wrist to elbow, like a ploughed field. But, through tears, Jaya sees she is still breathing.

Two workmen run to her side; they've heard the baby scream.

"*Arey, arey, Hai Bhagwan*, my God, what happened?" the man in a red turban asks, helplessly. But the other removes a fine muslin band from around his head, rips it in two, and ties one piece around Neelam's head.

"Keep your finger tight here," he tells Jaya. "Push down on it." Then he turns to his co-worker "*Pani, pani* Go bring cold water, you fool. Don't waste time calling God."

The bandage under Jaya's fingers gets red. "Can you get a

taxi? Is there a hospital near here?" she asks.

"The closest hospital is twenty miles away; it'll take too long."

Both men leave, rushing away into the thickets behind the road. Jaya looks down at the child in her lap. She can see a delicate network of veins on her closed eyelids, her mocha-colored glistening skin, her upturned palm indented with the looped pattern of chain links. Tenderly, she covers Neelam's exposed buttocks and picks a torn leaf from her hair. The bandage under her fingers is soaking red now. Gently, she peels it off and replaces it with the second strip of cloth. "Please God," she prays, closing her eyes. "What will you have from me? Ask it, ask anything you want. Just not this child—the only precious thing I have. I won't ask for anything more." She repeats the words mantra style, over and over, her lips moving, beaded tears quivering at the corners of her eyes. After awhile, the prayer dwindles to two words. "Please God, please God, please..."

She wishes she had worn a soft voile *sari* instead of a cotton *salwar khameez* shirt and pant, so difficult to convert into bandages. Afraid to draw her hand away from the child's forehead, she watches a mosquito land on her flesh, its jointed legs tickling the hair on her arm. Unable to slap it off, she watches the sting turn to a ripe, red berry.

Precious moments pass before her closed eyes, frame by frame. The day she'd boarded the bus and returned from Bombay, back home to her village, breathlessly running past the culvert, up the steps, scents of flowers and incense, murmurs of the women outside, the face of her sister, Seema, etched in pain and joy at the miraculous birth of this girl-child. The day they'd gone to the bus-stop to meet Vipul, Neelam's father, only to find he wasn't there, and wouldn't be, the next day, and the next. She sees the bus engine come round the bend, belching exhaust

216

fumes. She sees passengers descend, one by one, lugging children and baggage.

Sensing a presence, Jaya opens her eyes suddenly. The man in the turban has returned with a brass *lotah* filled with water. Cupping his big hand, he pours some water out, then makes a spout with his fingers and drizzles it over the child's head, carefully avoiding the gash. Neelam doesn't stir. He continues, as if anointing her, over and over, while Jaya whispers, "Neelam, baby, can you hear me? *Beti?* Daughter, open your eyes."

There is no answer. A puff of wind rises, swirling a few dried leaves, startling the sparrows congregated around the dripping water hose. Crows, undaunted by the weather, perch on the electric wire surveying the landscape for scraps of food left over by the construction workers. A crumpled piece of newspaper blows toward them. Jaya looks around in a daze. Two crows have found a banana peel and are chasing each other at the far end of the courtyard. They approach, nearing, scrambling, wrestling to tear it apart. Other crows join in the fray, as the cawing develops into an angry cacophony. Jaya pushes down the scream in her chest. It's like a horror movie—a child dying in her lap, angry, menacing black birds smelling blood, fighting on the sun-bleached ground, waiting. And Jaya is both acting in and watching these movie frames one by one.

In reality, Neelam's breathing is slowing, her feet are colder, and her lips seem bluer, but that must surely be because she's lying in the shade, and the wind has really picked up now, Jaya murmurs to herself. Yes, of course, that must be it. What other real reason can there be? she asks, in a fresh torrent of tears.

"*Arey, arey*, how much will you cry, sister?" the man asks, continuing to anoint Neelam. "Come now, your *butcha* will be alright."

"She's not really my child," Jaya says between sobs. "She is my sister's baby."

"Oh, oh," the man says, trying to engage her in conversation, "and where is your child?"

"I have no children—only this baby—my sister's. I—we—were just looking at this building…"

"Oh? Why were you looking at this building?"

She guesses he's trying to distract her further. "I was wondering if there was a vacancy," she says.

"Oh, a vacancy? I don't think so. Most of it is reserved or occupied, I'm sure." Seeing Jaya's eyes well up again, he continues, "But, who can say? No one tells us anything. We just go from site to site, following orders to build."

"Your friend?" Jaya says, her voice breaking. "Has he left? Abandoned us? This isn't going to work," she points to his water-anointing routine. "We must get to a hospital."

But barely has she uttered the words when he appears from across the street, walking awkwardly in big strides. In his hands, he carries two flat stones and a fistful of seedling plants. Sweat drips from his temples along a scar marking his jaw line. Without glancing at Jaya or his friend, he crouches and begins sorting out two types of leaves. He crushes the darker, thin leaves into a paste between two flat stones, and applies the leafy patty to Neelam's forehead. He tilts the *lotah*, rinses his fingers, then crushes the thicker, serrated leaves between his coarse fingers and waves them beneath Neelam's nostrils. Nothing happens. Jaya watches, her heart beating faster. The man continues calmly, crushing more leaves, his fingers gummy with sap. Jaya can smell them from where she sits, but Neelam's eyes remain closed.

Jaya's night is filled with ghosts. In her sleep she sees white angels lift

Neelam from the swing and carry her over the clouds up into a sky moth eaten with stars. A full moon rises higher and cuts a path on the earth below, where Jaya is now pushing an empty swing, urging Neelam to grab the rope and come back to her. She keeps pushing the swing higher and higher above the mourning trees, above the buildings and balconies, into the cloud-torn sky. She hears Neelam calling, her little brown hands reaching out, trying to grasp the rope, but she cannot hold on, and in a vivid collage of color, she disappears, as if the clouds at that moment, had split into a million prisms.

Jaya's eyes snap open to the early light of morning. Quickly, she tries to rise, but falls back into her pillow. Suddenly she is aware of aching arms and a head like a lead ball. Rubbing her palms to her wet cheeks, she realizes she's been weeping in her sleep. She closes her eyes again, breathes deeply, and lets the new morning seep slowly under her skin.

The events of yesterday return with clarity. Once Neelam regained consciousness, the medicine man, or the construction man, or whoever he was, had helped them into a taxi. She'd taken Neelam to the nearest emergency room at Ganesh Hospital, where they'd waited, like what seemed forever, to see a doctor. Amazingly, Neelam's X-rays showed no broken bones; her head had no fractures. The gash in her temple was sewn—it took twelve stitches, and she'd lost some blood. Her elbow and arm were skinned badly. In time it would it would heal, the doctor told Jaya. He'd given Neelam an antibiotic injection immediately, and a prescription for some tetra—cycle—something, which she'd filled right there at the hospital pharmacy. Fortunately, she always carried money with her in a little cloth pouch tucked at her waist.

Of course, Seema and Shanti were distraught when they got home from the hospital. What had possessed Jaya to take a two-year-old to an unfinished construction site?

"I didn't intend to," Jaya explained. "We went for a bus ride."

"Bus ride to Palghat?" Shanti almost spat the words out. "Why?"

Jaya hadn't answered. She knew that her mother knew exactly what had drawn her to Palghat. She knew that her mother still recalled fragments of her own dream, how once many moons ago, she'd said she wanted to live in Palghat up on the sixth floor; she'd wanted to touch the moon. Now, as then, Jaya had gazed at her mother's face and dropped the subject. There was enough heartache to fill the present without digging up the past.

Jaya opens her eyes now and fixes them on the ceiling, where a spider is sewing a veil in the corner. She watches its activity—the careful movements of its legs, back and forth, the measured restraint, the total immersion in the moment, in the task at hand. Yes, the gods had heard her plea for Neelam's life. She'd called out to them loud and clear and they'd obliged. Whatever the price, she'd be happy to pay up. What deal had been struck, she didn't yet know, but she'd received her half, her end of the bargain. And for now, that is all she cares to know.

From the little window above her cot she hears Seema's soothing voice. "Drink a little, *beti*," she says. "See, I put rose syrup in the milk." She hears Neelam whimpering, the clink of a teaspoon. "Drink just this little bit. It's nice and sweet."

Jaya smiles. She knows her sister must have crushed an antibiotic pill into the rose-milk. She remembers another morning, one like today. Then too, Neelam was ill. She'd had a slight fever, but both she and her mother were dressed beautifully— Seema in a soft white voile *sari* with a red paisley border, Neelam in a pretty embroidered *salvar khameez*. Around Seema's neck was her black and gold *mangal sutra* chain, the equivalent of wedding rings, and on her forehead, the round, red *tikka* of a married woman. At the door was her suitcase bulging with gifts—a beautiful *sari* and a little stainless steel snuffbox for Ma-ji, her mother-in-law, a saffron tie-dye *sari* and a dozen glass bangles in rainbow colors for Saroj, her sister-in-law, and soft linen shawls for her husband, Vipul, and his brother. Their tiny house had been swept clean; there was incense burning on the window ledge; the Tulsi plant had been watered. Shanti had washed the rice and lentils, ready to be cooked later, and grated the coconut. This was a special day, the day Vipul would arrive.

"Why don't you and Ma go to the bus stop? I'll wait here with Neelam. It's a hot day, plus I can steal a little extra time with my baby," Jaya had said, gently tickling the child.

"Jaya, stop it. She still has a mild temperature. And she's weak," Shanti had scolded.

Jaya ran her fingers under Neelam's feet and up her belly. "Weak? Where? Let me see. Are you weak here? Or here, or here?"

Neelam had giggled and her eyes had lit up. But Jaya's had misted over. What would she do when they left?

An hour later, Jaya left with her mother for the bus stop. Seema preferred to stay with Neelam, and coax her into nursing a little more, she said.

The bus from Tilgiri had arrived on time, but Vipul wasn't on it. People poured out like bees from a beehive into the afternoon sun. When Jaya asked the driver if he'd left any passengers behind for lack of space, he'd said no, not at all. They'd managed to squeeze every one in. How about at Tilgiri village? Jaya asked. Yes, yes, everyone who wished to board at Tilgiri had done so.

Well, that's okay, Jaya told Seema; perhaps Vipul had missed the bus. Perhaps a letter or a telegram would arrive by evening, or the next day, informing them of a new arrival date, possibly the following Friday. But no letter came that day, or the next.

A week later, a white envelope with small, slanted handwriting arrived. Jaya watched Seema slit open the envelope and read. Seema's eyes had welled with tears as she handed over the letter to her sister. "Not now," Jaya read. "Perhaps next *Divali*. I'm sorry, but it's better this way. Saroj is pregnant! And it's going to be a boy. Any one can tell by her shape. Ma-ji looks weary, but she is thrilled, almost like a child herself. I'll come for you and Neelam in a few months."

But he never did, and it had been impossible to contain the gossip in their community. Some people muttered they weren't surprised at all, others pretended it was only a temporary set back. "Don't worry," their neighbor had said to Seema, "let *his* mother cook for *him*. You stay here and enjoy *your* mother's cooking. He'll come."

But Jaya knew then, as she knows now, that that day will not come, and one day, Neelam will learn the awful truth. Her father has never seen her. He abandoned her. If only she could spare Neelam, *her* baby, the pain, or at least defer it for as long as possible, until Neelam was old enough to handle it. But was there ever a good time? Here in this parched village, where the women still gathered at the water well each morning and talked, the story would never die. But, what about Palghat? Jaya recalls Neelam's radiant face on the swings. That was only yesterday, and yet a lifetime had passed.

Quickly, Jaya rises, gets dressed and leaves the house, avoiding Seema and Neelam. She must hurry. She knows she has one last chance at the Palghat apartments, if it isn't too late already. Turning left at the gate, she crosses the railway tracks and continues along the curved roads flanked by rice fields. In the distance she sees smoke billowing from the factories as the late afternoon shifts begin work. There is a spicy taste in the air, the smell of sweat and grime. Past tea-colored huts, an abandoned rusted bicycle, and a bevy of girls playing hop-scotch in the dust. Jaya quickens her pace to the bus-stop.

By the time she arrives at Palghat, most of the construction workers have left. Standing not too far from where Neelam had fallen, Jaya shades her eyes and glances up at oval splashes of orange light bouncing off the sixth floor windows. Two workmen, looking like crows on a windowsill, are painting the last of the trim. Here, Jaya muses, they would have two rooms, one to cook and eat in, one to live and sleep in. At the end of each hallway, there'll be communal bathrooms and showers. No going to the old well anymore, no carrying *lotahs* of water to outdoor latrines. Here, they'll have a little verandah overlooking the courtyard. Jaya pictures Neelam swinging from monkey bars, jumping in the sand pit, even riding a bicycle one day. Why not? After all, this child makes her feel as close to being a mother as she'll ever be.

Turning away from the building, Jaya walks south on Guru Nanak Road toward a row of low roofed municipality buildings. If she hurries, she might get to the government office before they close for the day. Adjusting the strap of her sandal, she begins to take longer strides, deftly dodging idle cows and children at play. If she hurries, she can overtake that bullock cart piled high with sacks, most likely grain—*jowari*, or *bajra*, the poor man's wheat, or maybe green, tender coconuts en route to a beach or village fair. Walking faster and faster, she overtakes the bullock cart. She must get there soon. Why had she waited so long to make a decision? What if it was already too late?

The door to the office is ajar. From the corner, Jaya can see

223

shelves of dog-eared sheaves of paper bound with clips, rubber bands, or twine, and long, hard-cover ledgers, with dates block-printed on the spine. She approaches the nearest desk occupied by a woman who, anticipating Jaya's question, waves her to a sign, and then continues recording entries from a pile of loose notes into a red-bound ledger.

There isn't much to explain, Jaya says to the bespectacled man in a checked shirt and khaki pants. She's just late, that's all, but she really, truly wants to live at Palghat. The clerk, bored with his routine, looks up. Jaya flashes a smile and leans into the desk. Could she make an application for an apartment on the 6th floor?

"So late? There won't be vacancy," he says.

"Oh, please, please look again," Jaya begs, "there must be something." She knows that here in this dingy, stifling room, the clerk may as well be that humming table fan, or a clattering type-writer. If she flatters him, he just might oblige. "You seem like a kind man. I really need your help," she smiles.

It works. Opening a thick ledger, he begins paging back and forth, wetting his middle finger with spittle to flip stuck pages. With his index finger, he goes across and down a series of lines.

"Really Madam, they're all taken," he says.

"Oh, no—oh," Jaya says in a shocked, pained voice. "Oh, that's terrible." She looks as if she is about to burst into tears. She rummages in her bag for a spare handkerchief, but doesn't find a clean one. Instead, she finds a blue-lined one wrapped around a stack of banknotes, tied in a knot. Undoing the bundle, she sets the contents on the counter within full view of the clerk and wipes her eyes and lips.

"What about another floor?" she asks, idly beginning to count the stack of rupees, as if it were an urgent task she had overlooked. She flicks the notes expertly using her thumb and middle finger, one by one, her lips counting softly. From the corners of her eyes, she sees his thoughts sprouting like wild wheat. He resumes turning pages, working down rows of names and addresses, deposits, numbers with and without asterisks, some smudged.

Suddenly, he stops abruptly, his finger pressed to the bottom of a page. Noticing the hesitation, Jaya abandons her counting and leans forward. "Yes?" she says, "you found something?"

"Not really," he says. "First, I thought, but...."

Jaya is dubious. She flashes another smile and leans forward just a little. "I'm sure you will. I know you can," she says.

Jaya imagines his complaining wife—"Aiy, not now, not now, how much you want? I work all day planting rice, breaking my back. And you want to break it more?" She imagines him feeling spurned, frustrated. She knows he is aware of her standing there, the fresh wheat color of her skin, her mouth, and of course, the unspoken language of money. She knows his buttocks are clenched to stop the tingling.

"Madam," he says, looking up. "On fourth floor there is Mr. Shah from Gujarat state. He has only paid half deposit."

Jaya flashes another big smile. "He did? Well, now I can pay the full amount today itself. I can go home and bring it in one hour. And, I can bring more too," she adds, knowingly.

The clerk looks down at his ledger again. "One reminder notice was sent last week to Mr. Shah," he says, "money could be on the way, in today's post. Maybe, better I should wait."

Jaya says nothing. She knows there are times when a woman should be quiet. She knows the power of silence, of allowing him the feeling of control. She continues to stand near the desk, while he pretends to flip a few more pages. And just at the right moment, she raises her eyes to his, and holds his gaze, instinctively knowing that the game is all but over.

"Let me see what I can do, Madam," he says, a glint in his eye. "Can you come tomorrow?"

"Yes, of course," Jaya says, "what time?"

"Same time," he replies, "like today."

But Jaya knows that time doesn't matter. Tomorrow she'll return with the required deposit. In a separate envelope tucked discreetly in the folder, she'll include a generous bribe. This is the envelope he will slit open first, snapping the notes, counting. She knows he is no novice at this business, which is just the way all business is done.

On the way home once again, Jaya looks up at the sky—coral and lavender streaks in a blue expanse as the sun begins its rapid descent behind this little inlet of the Arabian Sea.

Shanti's mouth hangs open a full thirty seconds before she bursts out. She looks at the brown envelope and the stack of white typed carbon copies that Jaya has placed in her lap. Palghat, 4th Floor, number 28, in big bold letters, it says on the front. Inside there are pages and pages of writing with Jaya's signature on them. Other pages have drawings of the colony, their building and the surrounding ones, including the play area where Neelam had had her accident.

"What's this?" Shanti exclaims.

"Just what it says, Ma," Jaya replies.

"We're moving to Palghat?"

Jaya nods. Seema stands beside her mother in utter shock and silence. Her face is almost pale. "Are you crazy?" Shanti says, turning to Jaya. "How? We have no money."

"Yes, we do," Jaya replies calmly. "I paid nearly a third already. The rest is a government loan."

Shanti's eyes widen in disbelief. "Paid? You paid one third? How? Where did you get the money?"

"I earned it; I saved it, it's my money," Jaya says smoothly, firmly.

She is resolved not to elaborate further now or ever. Turning away toward the window, she waits for all of it to sink in. Outside, a handful of boys are playing cricket with bats and wickets whittled from tree trunks. Jaya watches the pitcher, a boy in a yellow T-shirt, swing his arm in a wide arc. The ball whizzes by the batsman as hoots and cheers rise from people squatted around. Someone shouts an obscenity. The pitcher takes up his position. In his hand, Jaya knows, is nothing more than a well-worn tennis ball. She recalls the many well-known cricketers who'd frequented Miraj Bar. She'd served them, listened to their conversations about cricket teams and boyhood dreams crystallized into hard cash. She'd seen the way they threw money around and soaked up the adulation of fans. These kids hooting and hollering here in the afternoon sun on a baked piece of earth would never feel the hard skin of a real cricket ball, and never know the difference.

Shanti's voice startles her. There is the slightest hint of excitement, a thread of hope. "And what if Neelam falls from the swing again?" she asks.

Jaya swivels on her heel, glad to switch gears. "Ma, she won't fall. She'll never fall. I won't push her hard again. I won't push the swing at all. Seema can take her out, only Seema, not me." She pauses to catch her breath. "Ma, be happy," she pleads, "for once. You deserve it. We deserve it," she smiles. "All four of us girls— it's time."

Shanti's eyes are misty as she looks at her daughter, this strange girl-child of hers, who wears the birthmark of a son.

GLOSSARY

Some of the words and phrases below are often casually incorporated into the English language by Indian people living in India and abroad. Most of them are borrowed from Hindi.

alloo	potato
amma	mother, a form of address
bajra	millet, ground and made into flat bread
beta; beti	son; daughter
bhaji	leafy vegetable
bindi	traditional or trendy, worn on the foreheads of Indian women
biryani	a spicy rice dish with meat or vegetables
brinjal	eggplant, aubergine
butcha	child, male or female

chai	tea
chapati	flat, wheat bread, like tortillas
chappals	sandals, footwear
choli	short, tightly fitted, complimentary blouse worn with saris
chota bhai	younger brother
chuddi	term for underpants
coolie	luggage porter
dal	lentil soup or curry
Divali	Indian Festival of Lights — as important to Hindus as Christmas is to Christians.
dhobhi	washerman or woman
ghee	clarified butter, rich and delicious
gul-mohur	tree with orange and yellow blossoms
hai bhagwan	Oh God; Good Lord, a common expression
halwa	an aromatic sweet Indian dessert; comes in different flavors and textures.
jaggery	a type of brown sugar processed from sugarcane
jambool	a purple tropical fruit
jowari	around seed (grain), ground and rolled into flat bread

kaftan	a long, loose garment
kajal	black paste eyeliner
kebab	grilled chunks of marinated meat or fish
kesar	orange stigma of a species of crocus, exotic Asian spice
khali	empty
kismet	fate, destiny
kurta	shirt-like, slightly loose-fitting garment
lassi	thick milk-yogurt based drink; comes in flavors
lotah	round urn used to carry water
masala	a paste of spices and herbs; stone-ground
memsahib/ sahib	respectful forms of address to the lady and man of the house, respectively.
mehndi	henna to color hair and skin
mora	wide-backed cane chair
mori	area for bathing or washing
namaste	hands joined in a form of greeting in India
nankatai	a sweet, similar to a cookie
nans	baked, leavened, white flour Indian bread
neem	common Indian medicinal tree
paise	Indian currency

pakora	fritter dipped in spicy chickpea batter
pani	water
palloo	one end of six yards of a *sari*
pulao	aromatic rice pilaf
peepul	a species of fig tree with religious significance
phool walla	flower vendor
puja	prayer ceremony
puri	palm-sized, airy, deep-fried bread
roti	thin bread cooked on griddle
salaam	Indian salute
salwar khameez	pants and tunic
samosa	spicy potato, wrapped in balls of dough
sari	six yards of material, draped different ways
sindhur	red powder worn in the parting of a married woman's hair
thali	round, flat tray on which food is eaten, or served.
tonga	horse-drawn carriage
tulsi	basil plant, venerated in India
vati	small, round container
sundari	pretty girl

ACKNOWLEDGMENTS

Lawrence F. Blob, my husband of thirty-one years, my friend;

Jonathan and Anjali, our children, my toughest, most loved literary critics;

Agnes Noronha, my mother, another perceptive critic, for her magic pen and bright ideas;

Hildreth D. Noronha, my brother and computer guru, for believing I could write;

Zarina Noronha Smith, my sister, for her unwavering love and encouragement;

Susan Muaddi Darraj, Barbara Diehl, Danuta E. Kosik-Kosicka and Patricia Schultheis, my writer's group, for their sharp eyes and warmth;

The Ragdale Foundation and the Maryland State Arts Council, for their support of this work.

Michon Lartigue, my editor, for her insight, and Kwame Alexander, my publisher, for his leap of faith in our journey.

Thank you with all my heart.

ABOUT THE AUTHOR

Born in Bombay, Lalita Noronha came to the USA on a Fulbright travel grant and earned her Ph.D in Microbiology. Her literary work has been widely published in The Christian Science Monitor, Catholic Digest, Crab Orchard Review, The Baltimore Sun, Potomac Review, and other journals and anthologies. She is the recipient of the Maryland Literary Arts Award for Short Story and a Maryland State Arts Council Individual Artist Award for Fiction. Currently working on her first novel, she resides in Baltimore, Maryland, where she is a fiction editor for The Baltimore Review, and a science teacher at St. Paul's School for Girls.